JACK LONDON'S

THE CALL OF THE WILD

THE GRAPHIC NOVEL

adapted by **Neil Kleid**

illustrated by **Alex Niño**

PUFFIN BOOKS

PUFFIN BOOKS
Published by the Penguin Group
Penguin Young Readers Group,
345 Hudson Street, New York, NY 10014 U.S.A.
Penguin Group (Canada), 90 Eglinton Avenue East, Suite 700,
Toronto, Ontario, Canada M4P 2Y3 (a division of Pearson Penguin Canada Inc.)
Penguin Books Ltd, 80 Strand, London WC2R 0RL, England
Penguin Ireland, 25 St. Stephen's Green, Dublin 2, Ireland
(a division of Penguin Books Ltd)
Penguin Group (Australia), 250 Camberwell Road, Camberwell, Victoria 3124,
Australia (a division of Pearson Australia Group Pty Ltd)
Penguin Books India Pvt Ltd, 11 Community Centre, Panchsheel Park,
New Delhi – 110 017, India
Penguin Group (NZ), Cnr Airborne and Rosedale Roads, Albany, Auckland 1310,
New Zealand (a division of Pearson New Zealand Ltd)
Penguin Books (South Africa) (Pty) Ltd, 24 Sturdee Avenue, Rosebank,
Johannesburg 2196, South Africa

Registered Offices: Penguin Books Ltd, 80 Strand, London WC2R 0RL, England

First published by Puffin Books, a division of Penguin Young Readers Group, 2006

10 9 8 7 6 5 4 3 2

Copyright © Byron Preiss Visual Publications, 2006
All rights reserved

A Byron Preiss Book
Byron Preiss Visual Publications
24 West 25th Street, New York, NY 10010

Adapted by Neil Kleid
Illustrated by Alex Niño
Cover art by Alex Niño
Lettering by M. Postawa, Brendan Diaz, Raul Carvajal
Series Editor: Dwight Jon Zimmerman
Series Assistant Editor: April Isaacs
Interior design by Gilda Hannah, M. Postawa, and Raul Carvajal
Cover design by M. Postawa

Puffin Books ISBN 0-14-240571-X

Printed in the United States of America

THE CALL OF THE WILD

OLD LONGINGS NOMADIC LEAP

CHAFING AT CUSTOM'S CHAIN

AGAIN FROM ITS BRUMAL SLEEP

WAKENS THE FERINE STRAIN

MEN, GROPING IN THE *ARCTIC DARKNESS*, HAD DISCOVERED *GOLD* ALONG THE WHITE NORTH.

THEY WANTED *DOGS*--DOGS WITH MUSCLES TO WORK AND *COATS* TO KEEP OUT WINTER'S CHILL.

THEY WANTED *FAST DOGS.* HEAVY DOGS.

DOGS LIKE *BUCK.*

BUCK LIVED AT A BIG HOUSE IN THE *SANTA CLARA VALLEY.* JUDGE MILLER'S PLACE, IT WAS CALLED.

HALF-HIDDEN AMONG THE TREES, *LAWNS,* STABLES, AND CEMENT TANK KEPT THE JUDGE'S BOYS *REFRESHED* ON HOT AFTERNOONS.

AND OVER THIS GREAT HOUSE, *BUCK* RULED.

THERE WERE *OTHER DOGS*, TRUE; FROM PAMPERED JAPANESE *PUGS* THAT RARELY LEFT THE HOUSE...

...TO *TERRIERS* WHO YELPED THREATS FROM BEHIND THE *WINDOWS*.

BUT BUCK WAS THE UNDISPUTED *LORD OF THE REALM*.

HE *HUNTED* WITH THE JUDGE'S SONS AND *ESCORTED* HIS DAUGHTERS ON LONG TWILIGHT RAMBLES.

HIS *FATHER* HAD BEEN THE JUDGE'S *COMPANION,* AND BUCK UPHELD HIS LEGACY.

HUNTING KEPT HIM *LEAN* AND THE OUTDOORS KEPT HIM *FIT.* PRIDEFUL AND A TRIFLE EGOTISTICAL, BUCK LIVED A LIFE OF *EASE.*

THIS WAS BUCK IN THE FALL OF *1897,* AS MEN TOILED AND DREAMED IN THE *FROZEN NORTH.*

ONE NIGHT, BUCK WENT FOR A *STROLL* WITH THE *GARDENER'S HELPER* TO THE LOCAL TRAIN STATION.

THEY WERE MET BY A *SOLITARY MAN* AND *MONEY* CHANGED HANDS.

TWIST THE *ROPE* AN' YOU'LL CHOKE 'IM.

BUCK ACCEPTED IT, *TRUSTING* HIS MASTER'S MAN. BUT THINGS *CHANGED* WHEN HE HANDED OVER THE ROPE.

BUCK GROWLED HIS DISPLEASURE. TO HIS SURPRISE THE ROPE TIGHTENED AROUND HIS NECK, SHUTTING OFF HIS BREATH.

NEVER IN ALL HIS LIFE HAD HE BEEN SO VILELY TREATED, AND NEVER IN ALL HIS LIFE HAD HE BEEN SO ANGRY.

THE MAN GRAPPLED HIM BY THE THROAT, AND WITH A TWIST THREW HIM OVER ON HIS BACK.

BUCK *STRUGGLED* AND PANTED, BUT THE MEN *OVERPOWERED* HIM.

HIS STRENGTH *FAILED*, HIS EYES GLAZED...

...AND THE NEXT THING HE KNEW WAS DARKNESS.

BUCK WOKE TO
THE SOUND OF
A *STEAM
WHISTLE.*

UPON OPENING HIS
EYES, HIS ANGER
SWELLED LIKE A
KIDNAPPED KING.

BUCK'S *JAWS* CLOSED ON THE
STRANGER'S HAND AND DID
NOT *RELAX* UNTIL HIS SENSES
WERE CHOKED OUT OF HIM
ONCE MORE.

BUCK WAS *SOLD* IN A SAN FRANCISCO SALOON THAT VERY NIGHT.

HIS TORMENTORS FILED THE BRASS COLLAR OFF HIS NECK, AND HE WAS FLUNG INTO A CAGE-LIKE CRATE.

THERE HE LAY, NURSING HIS WRATH AND WOUNDED PRIDE. WHAT DID THEY WANT WITH HIM?

IN THE MORNING, HE BEGAN A *TWO-DAY JOURNEY* FROM TRUCK TO *STEAMER* TO EXPRESS CAR.

FOR TWO DAYS AND NIGHTS BUCK NEITHER ATE NOR DRANK. DURING THAT TORMENT, HE WAS METAMORPHOSED INTO A RAGING FIEND.

FINALLY, BUCK WAS DELIVERED INTO THE HANDS OF A *MAN* WITH A SAGGING *RED SWEATER.*

ANSWERS TO *BUCK.* YOU AIN'T GOIN' TO TAKE HIM *OUT,* ARE YOU?

SURE.

THE MEN *SCATTERED* AS BUCK TORE AT THE SPLINTERED *WOOD,* ANXIOUS TO *ATTACK* HIS LATEST TORMENTOR.

NOW, YOU *RED-EYED DEVIL...*

HE HAD NEVER FELT A *CLUB* BEFORE. JUST AS HIS JAWS WERE ABOUT TO CLOSE ON THE MAN, HE RECEIVED A SHOCK THAT CHECKED HIS BODY WITH AN AGONIZING CLIP.

THE CLUB *BROKE* BUCK'S *CHARGE.*

AND MADNESS BROUGHT HIM BACK FOR *MORE.* HE WAS *AWARE* OF THE CLUB, BUT STILL HE *FOUGHT,* WITH A SNARL THAT WAS PART BARK, PART *SCREAM.*

AGAIN AND *AGAIN* BUCK CHARGED, AND THE *CLUB* WAS ALWAYS THERE.

THE MAN *STRUCK* THE SHREWD BLOW HE HAD WITHHELD FOR SO LONG, AND BUCK *LAY* WHERE HE FELL.

STRENGTH *DRAINED,* HE SLOWLY BECAME *AWARE* OF THE MAN IN THE SWEATER AT HIS SIDE.

WELL, *BUCK,* MY BOY...WE'LL *LEAVE* IT AT THAT.

YOU'VE *LEARNED* YOUR PLACE, AND I KNOW MINE. BE A *GOOD DOG...*

...AND WE'LL *GET ALONG* FINE.

BUCK WAS BEATEN, BUT HE WAS NOT BROKEN.

THAT CLUB WAS A REVELATION.

IT WAS HIS INTRODUCTION TO THE REIGN OF PRIMITIVE LAW AND HE FACED IT UNCOWED.

AS THE DAYS PASSED, BUCK WATCHED OTHER DOGS COME AND PASS UNDER
THE DOMINION OF THE MAN IN THE SWEATER. AND BUCK LEARNED THAT A MAN
WITH A CLUB WAS A MASTER TO BE *OBEYED;* THOUGH NOT NECESSARILY LOVED.

NOW AND AGAIN, *STRANGERS* ARRIVED AND TRADED *MONEY* FOR TWO OR
THREE *DOGS.* BUCK WONDERED WHERE THEY WENT, FOR THEY NEVER CAME
BACK. THE FEAR OF THE FUTURE WAS STRONG UPON HIM, AND HE WAS GLAD
EACH TIME WHEN HE WAS NOT SELECTED.

YET HIS TIME
CAME IN THE
FORM OF A
*GOVERNMENT
COURIER* NAMED
PERRAULT,
LOOKING FOR
DOGS TO PULL
HIS SLED.

PERRAULT
PURCHASED
BUCK AND A
DOG NAMED
CURLY.

AND THAT WAS THE *LAST*
BUCK SAW OF THE MAN IN
THE RED SWEATER.

18

AND THAT WAS THE LAST HE SAW OF THE WARM *SOUTHLAND.* PERRAULT TOOK THE DOGS BELOW THE DECK OF THE *NARWHAL,* AND THEN TO *SEA.*

THEY WERE GIVEN INTO THE *CARE* OF A FRENCH-CANADIAN HALF-BREED NAMED *FRANCOIS.* PERRAULT AND FRANCOIS WERE A NEW KIND OF MEN TO BUCK.

AND WHILE HE FELT NO *LOVE* FOR THEM, HE GREW TO *RESPECT* THEM. THEY WERE *WISE* IN THE WAY OF DOGS AND *FAIR* TO JUDGE.

BUCK AND CURLY JOINED *TWO OTHER DOGS* ABOARD THE *NARWHAL.*

ONE, A HUSKY NAMED *SPITZ,* WAS FRIENDLY, IN A TREACHEROUS WAY. AT THE FIRST MEAL, HE *STOLE* BUCK'S FOOD, EARNING HIM BUCK'S SNARL AND FRANCOIS'S WHIP.

THE OTHER WAS *GLOOMY* AND MOROSE. HE MADE IT CLEAR HE WISHED TO BE ALONE.

HE WAS CALLED *DAVE,* AND HE ATE AND SLEPT, TAKING INTEREST IN NOTHING AND NO ONE.

THOUGH ONE DAY WAS VERY LIKE ANOTHER, IT WAS APPARENT TO BUCK THAT THE WEATHER WAS STEADILY GROWING COLDER.

AT LAST, ONE MORNING THE PROPELLER WAS QUIET. FRANCOIS LEASHED THE DOGS AND BROUGHT THEM *ABOVE DECK.*

BUCK'S FEET *SANK* INTO A COLD, WHITE MUSHY *SOMETHING* LIKE MUD.

MORE OF THIS WHITE STUFF *FELL* THROUGH THE AIR, COVERING HIS COAT WITH A FINE, *WHITE DUST.*

HE LICKED SOME ON HIS *TONGUE* AND IT BIT LIKE *FIRE,* BUT THE NEXT INSTANT WAS *GONE.*

FRANÇOIS AND THE ONLOOKERS *LAUGHED* AS BUCK TRIED IT AGAIN, AND HE FELT ASHAMED.

HE DIDN'T KNOW WHY THEY *LAUGHED.* IT WAS HIS *FIRST SNOW.*

THROUGH IT ALL, THE *NARWHAL* CONTINUED ITS JOURNEY TO THE PORT OF DYEA.

BUCK'S FIRST DAY ON THE DYEA BEACH WAS LIKE A *NIGHTMARE*. HERE WAS NEITHER PEACE, REST, NOR A MOMENT'S *SAFETY*.

ALL WAS CONFUSION AND ACTION, AND EVERY MOMENT LIFE AND LIMB WERE IN PERIL.

THE MEN AND DOGS OF THE CAMP WERE *SAVAGES* WHO KNEW NO LAW BUT THAT OF CLUB AND *FANG*.

HE HAD NEVER SEEN DOGS FIGHT AS THESE WOLFISH CREATURES FOUGHT. HIS FIRST EXPERIENCE TAUGHT HIM AN UNFORGETTABLE LESSON.

ONE THAT COST CURLY HER *LIFE*.

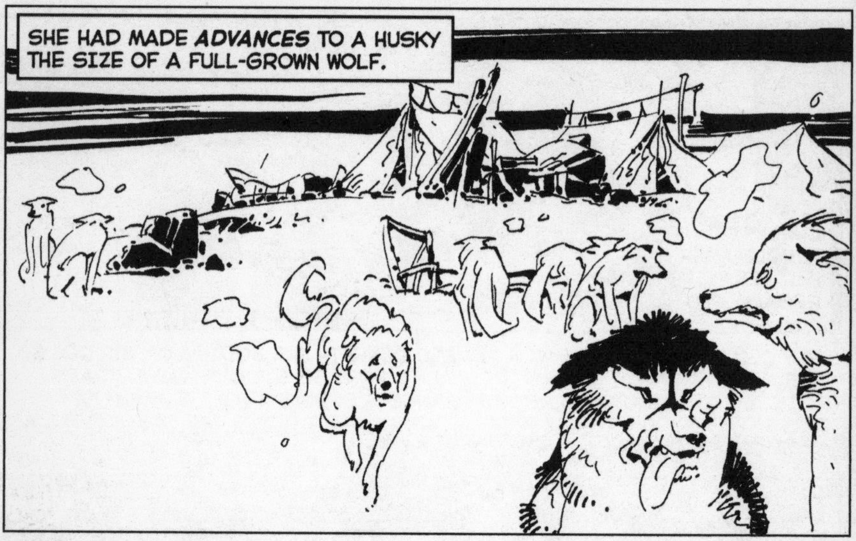
SHE HAD MADE *ADVANCES* TO A HUSKY THE SIZE OF A FULL-GROWN WOLF.

THERE WAS NO *WARNING,* ONLY A LEAP IN LIKE A FLASH AND CURLY'S FACE WAS RIPPED OPEN. IT WAS THE WOLF MANNER OF FIGHTING--STRIKE AND LEAP AWAY.

A SILENT *CIRCLE* OF HUSKIES SURROUNDED THE *COMBATANTS,* PENNING THEM IN.

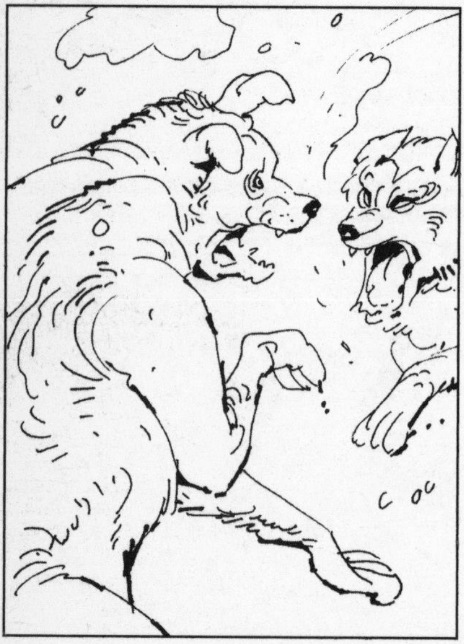

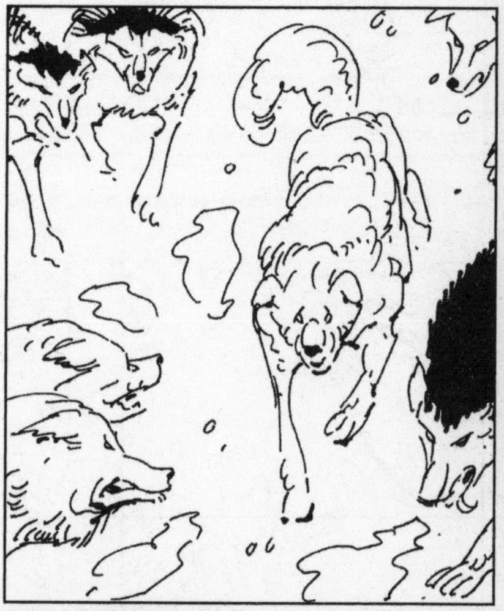

BUCK DID NOT UNDERSTAND THE *INTENT,* OR THE EAGER WAY THE HUSKIES LICKED THEIR *CHOPS.*

CURLY'S *ENEMY* TUMBLED HER OFF HER FEET. SHE NEVER REGAINED THEM.

THEY CLOSED IN AND SHE WAS *BURIED* BENEATH THE BODIES OF THE DOGS. THIS WAS WHAT THE HUSKIES HAD WAITED FOR. SO SUDDEN WAS IT THAT BUCK WAS TAKEN ABACK. HE SAW FRANCOIS SPRING INTO THE *MESS* OF *DOGS.* TWO MINUTES FROM THE TIME CURLY WENT DOWN, THE LAST OF THEM WERE CLUBBED OFF.

HE SAW SPITZ RUN HIS *TONGUE* OUT, IN A WAY HE HAD OF LAUGHING, AND BUCK *HATED* HIM WITH A BITTER, DEATHLESS HATRED.

SO THAT WAS THE WAY. NO *FAIR PLAY.* HE WOULD SEE TO IT THAT HE NEVER WENT DOWN.

IN THE MORNING, BUCK RECEIVED ANOTHER *SHOCK* WHEN FRANCOIS FASTENED A *HARNESS* TO HIS NECK AND SET HIM TO *WORK*.

THOUGH IS *DIGNITY* WAS SORELY HURT, HE WAS TOO WISE TO *REBEL*. HE DID HIS BEST, THOUGH IT WAS ALL NEW AND STRANGE.

FRANCOIS WAS *STERN*, CORRECTING THE DOGS WITH HIS *WHIP*.

DAVE AND SPITZ CORRECTED HIS *ERRORS* BY NIPPING HIM FROM BEHIND OR THROWING *WEIGHT* FROM THE FRONT, RESPECTIVELY.

BUCK *LEARNED* EASILY, AND UNDER THE *TUITION* OF HIS MATES AND FRANCOIS MADE REMARKABLE *PROGRESS.*

HE KNEW TO STOP AT *"HO"*, MOVE AT *"MUSH"*, SWING WIDE AT BENDS, AND KEEP CLEAR OF THE WHEELER ON *DOWNHILL RUNS.*

T'REE VAIR' *GOOD DOGS.* BUCK, HIM PULL LIKE *HELL.* I TEACH HIM QUICK AS ANY'TING.

PERRAULT WAS IN A HURRY TO BE ON THE TRAIL. BY AFTERNOON HE RETURNED WITH BILLEE AND JOE, TWO BROTHERS, AND TRUE HUSKIES BOTH.

BILLEE WAS GOOD NATURED WHILE JOE WAS SOUR AND INTROSPECTIVE. SPITZ THRASHED AND BIT BILLEE, BUT LEFT JOE ALONE AFTER A *STAND OFF.*

BY EVENING, PERRAULT SECURED AN *OLD HUSKY,* SCARRED AND BLIND IN ONE EYE. HIS NAME WAS *SOL-LEKS,* MEANING "THE ANGRY ONE."

HE ASKED NOTHING, GAVE NOTHING, EXPECTED *NOTHING;* AND WHEN HE MARCHED SLOWLY INTO THEIR MIDST, EVEN SPITZ LEFT HIM ALONE.

HE DID NOT LIKE TO BE APPROACHED ON HIS *BLIND SIDE,* AND HIS COMRADES LET HIM BE.

THAT *NIGHT*, BUCK FACED THE PROBLEM OF SLEEPING.

BARRED FROM THE *TENTS*, HE LAY ON THE SNOW BUT THE FROST SOON DROVE HIM TO HIS FEET. MISERABLE, HE RETURNED TO SEE HOW HIS *TEAMMATES* WERE MAKING OUT. TO HIS ASTONISHMENT, THEY HAD DISAPPEARED.

SUDDENLY, THE SNOW GAVE WAY AND HE *SANK DOWN.* WARM AIR ASCENDED AND A FRIENDLY *YELP* SPLIT THE NIGHT.

THERE LAY *BILLEE,* SNUG UNDER THE SNOW. BUCK SELECTED A SPOT, DUG A *HOLE* AND SOUNDLY *SLEPT* IN THE RAPIDLY WARMING SPACE.

IN THE MORNING, BUCK *FORGOT* WHERE HE WAS. IT HAD SNOWED AND HE WAS COMPLETELY *BURIED.*

FEAR SWEPT THROUGH HIM AND HE BOUNDED UP TO *DAYLIGHT* AND THE WHITE CAMP.

HE SAW THE CAMP SPREAD BEFORE HIM AND *REMEMBERED* ALL THAT HAD PASSED SINCE SANTA CLARA.

THREE MORE *HUSKIES* WERE ADDED, AND THEY MADE READY TO LEAVE FOR *DAWSON.* SOON THEY WERE IN HARNESS AND UP THE TRAIL, TOWARDS THE DYEA CANYON.

BUCK WAS SURPRISED AT THE EAGERNESS WHICH ANIMATED THE TEAM.

THEY WERE NEW DOGS, TRANSFORMED BY THE *HARNESS.*

THE *TOIL* OF THE TRACES SEEMED ALL THEY LIVED FOR. AND THOUGH THE *WORK* WAS HARD...

...BUCK FOUND THAT HE DID NOT *HATE* IT.

DAVE WAS WHEELER, OR SLED DOG. PULLING IN FRONT OF HIM WAS BUCK, THEN CAME SOL-LEKS. THE REST OF THE TEAM STRUNG OUT AHEAD SINGLE FILE TO SPITZ, THE LEADER.

BUCK WAS PLACED BETWEEN DAVE AND SOL-LEKS TO RECEIVE *INSTRUCTION.* THEY WERE FAIR AND WISE.

FRANCOIS'S WHIP BACKED UP THEIR *HIPS* AND BUCK FOUND IT CHEAPER TO MEND HIS WAYS. BY DAY'S END BOTH HIS MATES AND THE WHIP CEASED *NAGGING* HIM.

IT WAS A *HARD DAY'S RUN,* ACROSS GLACIERS AND DRIFTS. LATE THAT NIGHT, THEY REACHED THE LAKE BENNETT *CAMP* AND BUCK DUG HIS HOLE ONCE MORE.

ALL TOO EARLY HE WAS ROUTED OUT AND HARNESSED WITH HIS MATES.

FOR DAYS THEY TOILED...HALTING AT DARK, SETTING OUT AT DAWN. BUCK WATCHED AND *LEARNED.*

WHEN PIKE, ONE OF THE NEW DOGS, STOLE *BACON* FROM PERRAULT, BUCK REPEATED THE PERFORMANCE...AND ANOTHER DOG WAS *BLAMED.*

BUCK ADAPTED TO THE *LAW* OF CLUB AND *FANG.* GONE WAS THE SOUTH-LAND DOG.

CLUB AND TRACE HAD BEATEN INTO HIM A MORE FUNDAMENTAL AND *PRIMITIVE* CODE.

INSTINCTS LONG DEAD BECAME *ALIVE* ONCE MORE.

THE OLD LIFE QUICKENED WITHIN HIM, THE *ANCIENT SONG* SURGING IN HIS VEINS.

AND ON STILL COLD NIGHTS HE *HOWLED* LONG AND WOLFLIKE--AND HIS ANCESTORS, DEAD AND DUST, THROUGH HIM.

HOWLING THROUGH THE CENTURIES.

THE PRIMORDIAL *BEAST* WAS STRONG IN BUCK. HIS NEW-BORN CUNNING GAVE HIM CONTROL AND HE NOT ONLY DID NOT PICK FIGHTS, BUT AVOIDED THEM. AND IN THE BITTER HATRED BETWEEN HIM AND SPITZ, HE SHOWED NO IMPATIENCE.

DRIVING *WIND* FORCED THEM TO CAMP ON THE *ICE* OF LAKE LE BARGE. FRANCOIS THAWED FISH OVER THE *FIRE*.

BUCK EMERGED FROM HIS NEST TO *EAT*. ONCE FINISHED, HE RETURNED TO FIND HIS *SHELTER* OCCUPIED.

THE TRESPASSER WAS *SPITZ*.

TILL NOW BUCK HAD AVOIDED TROUBLE, BUT THIS WAS TOO MUCH. THE BEAST IN HIM ROARED.

THEY SHOT OUT IN A FURIOUS *TANGLE* FROM THE DISRUPTED NEST.

THEN, MATTERS PROJECTED THEIR *STRUGGLE* FOR SUPREMACY FAR INTO THE FUTURE. *STARVING HUSKIES* HAD SCENTED THE CAMP AND CREPT IN DURING THE FIGHT, CRAZED BY THE SMELL OF FOOD. THE CLUBS FELL ON THEM UNHEEDED.

IN AN INSTANT, THE FAMISHED BRUTES SCRAMBLED FOR THE FOOD, TILL EVERY LAST CRUMB WAS DEVOURED.

THE TEAM DOGS, FIGHTING FIERCELY, WERE SWEPT BACK AT THE FIRST ONSET. THE WARM *BLOOD* IN BUCK'S MOUTH GOADED HIM ON.

AND THEN *TEETH* SANK INTO HIS *THROAT*...SPITZ, TREACHEROUSLY *ATTACKING* FROM THE SIDE.

BUCK SHOOK HIMSELF FREE AND JOINED HIS MATES IN THEIR *FLIGHT* OUT ON THE LAKE.

SPITZ RUSHED, INTENT ON OVERTHROWING HIM, BUT BUCK WAS DETERMINED NOT TO *FALL.* HE CONTINUED ACROSS THE *LAKE,* ANGER SWELLING AGAINST SPITZ.

THEY SOUGHT *SHELTER* IN THE FOREST AND LIMPED BACK AT DAYBREAK. THERE WAS NOT ONE WHO WAS NOT WOUNDED IN FOUR OR FIVE PLACES.

JOE HAD LOST AN EYE AND BILLEE'S EAR WAS *TORN.* DOLLY, THE LAST HUSKY FROM DYEA BEACH, HAD A TORN THROAT. FULLY HALF OF THEIR GRUB WAS GONE. NOTHING HAD ESCAPED THE MARAUDERS.

AH, MEBBE T'OSE BITES MAKE YOU ALL *MAD DOGS,* EH?

WHAT YOU T'INK?

PERRAULT SEEMED *DUBIOUS.* WITH FOUR HUNDRED MILES OF TRAIL TO DAWSON, HE COULD ILL AFFORD MADNESS AMONG THE DOGS.

TWO HOURS OF CURSING AND EXERTION AND THE WOUND-STIFFENED TEAM PAINFULLY STRUGGLED OVER THE HARDEST PART OF THE TRAIL THEY HAD YET ENCOUNTERED...

THE **WATER** OF THE THIRTY-MILE RIVER DEFIED THE **FROST**, ICE WEAK BENEATH THEIR FEET.

ONCE, THE SLED BROKE THROUGH WITH DAVE AND BUCK, AND THEY WERE **HALF-FROZEN** WHEN THEY WERE DRAGGED OUT.

FRANCOIS KEPT THEM RUNNING BY THE FIRE, THAWING AS THEY WENT.

AT ANOTHER TIME, SPITZ BROKE THROUGH, DRAGGING THE WHOLE TEAM AFTER HIM. BUCK AND DAVE STRAINED TO **SAVE** THEM, PAWS SLIDING ON THE ICE.

THE RIM ICE BROKE AWAY AND THERE WAS NO ESCAPE EXCEPT UP THE CLIFF.

PERRAULT SCALED THE WALL AND THE DOGS WERE *HOISTED*, ONE BY ONE, WITH FRANCOIS AND SLED FOLLOWING.

TO MAKE UP FOR *LOST TIME*...

...PERRAULT *PUSHED* THEM LATE AND EARLY.

THE DOGS WERE PLAYED OUT, BUT IN THREE DAYS COVERED ONE HUNDRED AND TEN MILES.

ONE MORNING, DOLLY WENT *MAD.*

SHE SPRANG STRAIGHT FOR BUCK. HE HAD NEVER SEEN A DOG GO MAD AND DID NOT HAVE REASON TO FEAR MADNESS; YET HE KNEW THERE WAS HORROR AND FLED IN *PANIC.*

SHE GAVE CHASE, JUST ONE LEAP BEHIND.

FRANCOIS APPEARED AND BUCK RAN, PUTTING HIS FAITH IN THAT FRANCOIS WOULD SAVE HIM.

THE DOG-DRIVER'S AXE CRASHED DOWN ON DOLLY'S HEAD.

BUCK *STAGGERED* FOR BREATH AND SPITZ CHOSE HIS MOMENT...

HE SPRANG, HIS TEETH TORE INTO HIS FOE, SINKING TO THE BONE.

THEN FRANCOIS'S LASH DESCENDED...

SPITZ RECEIVED THE WORST *WHIPPING* AS YET GIVEN TO ANY OF THEM.

ONE *DEVIL*, THAT SPITZ. SOME DAY HE'LL *KILL* BUCK.

DAT BUCK *TWO* DEVILS. ONE DAY HE GET *MAD* LIKE HELL...

...CHEW DAT SPITZ ALL UP AN' SPIT HIM ON DE SNOW.

IT WAS INEVITABLE THE CLASH FOR LEADERSHIP WOULD COME. BUCK WANTED IT. FROM THEN ON IT WAS WAR.

HE WANTED IT BECAUSE IT WAS HIS NATURE, BECAUSE HE HAD BEEN GRIPPED BY THE PRIDE OF THE TRAIL AND TRACE.

THE *PRIDE* WHICH HOLDS DOGS IN THE TOIL TO THE LAST GASP. THE *PRIDE* OF DAVE AS WHEEL-DOG; OF SOL-LEKS, PULLING WITH ALL HIS MIGHT.

THIS PRIDE BORE UP SPITZ, MAKING HIM THRASH SHIRKING DOGS. IT WAS HIS PRIDE THAT MADE HIM FEAR BUCK AS A POSSIBLE LEAD DOG.

AND THIS WAS *BUCK'S PRIDE,* TOO.

BUCK OPENLY THREATENED HIS FOE'S LEADERSHIP. HE CAME BETWEEN HIM AND THE SHIRKS HE SHOULD HAVE PUNISHED.

AND HE DID IT DELIBERATELY.

ONCE, WHEN SPITZ FLEW TO PUNISH PIKE, BUCK STEPPED BETWEEN WITH EQUAL *RAGE,* AND SPRANG UPON SPITZ.

IN THE FOLLOWING DAYS, BUCK *INTERFERED* BETWEEN SPITZ AND HIS MATES. AND WITH HIS COVERT MUTINY, *INSUBORDINATION* INCREASED.

THE REST OF THE TEAM WENT FROM BAD TO *WORSE*.

TROUBLE WAS ALWAYS AFOOT, AND AT THE BOTTOM OF IT WAS BUCK.

HE KEPT FRANCOIS BUSY, FOR THE DRIVER WAS ALWAYS IN CONSTANT APPREHENSION OF THE STRUGGLE BETWEEN THE TWO WHICH HE KNEW MUST TAKE PLACE SOONER OR LATER.

AND SO THEY PULLED INTO DAWSON ONE AFTERNOON WITH THE *GREAT FIGHT* STILL TO COME.

IN *DAWSON*, THE DOGS WERE PUT TO *WORK* HAULING LOGS TO THE MINES.

HERE AND THERE WERE SOUTHLAND DOGS, BUT IN THE MAIN THEY WERE A WILD WOLF HUSKY BREED.

EVERY NIGHT, REGULARLY AT NIGHT, AT TWELVE, AT THREE, THEY LIFTED A NOCTURNAL SONG, IN WHICH IT WAS BUCK'S DELIGHT TO JOIN.

IT WAS AN *OLD SONG*, OLD AS THE BREED ITSELF.

IT STIRRED HIM, HARKING BACK PAST THE *AGE OF FIRE* TO THE BEGINNINGS OF LIFE.

WITHIN SEVEN DAYS THEY DROPPED BACK DOWN THE *TRAIL* TO DYEA BEACH. PERRAULT PURPOSED TO MAKE A *RECORD TRIP,* CONDITIONS FAVORING THEIR RUN.

THEY COVERED GROUND, BUT BUCK'S *REVOLT* HAD DESTROYED THE SOLIDARITY OF THE TEAM.

NO MORE WAS SPITZ A LEADER TO BE *FEARED.* THE OLD AWE DEPARTED AND THE OTHERS GREW EQUAL TO *CHALLENGING* HIS AUTHORITY.

THE BREAKING DOWN OF DISCIPLINE
LIKEWISE AFFECTED THE DOGS IN THEIR
RELATIONS WITH ONE ANOTHER.

FRANCOIS BACKED SPITZ WITH HIS
WHIP WHILE BUCK BACKED THE
TEAM. AND HIS LASH WAS ALWAYS
SINGING, BUT IT WAS OF SMALL AVAIL.
FRANCOIS SWORE FRUSTRATED
OATHS.

FRANCOIS KNEW BUCK WAS BEHIND
THE TROUBLE, BUT BUCK WAS TOO
CLEVER TO BE CAUGHT.

HE WORKED *HARD* BUT TOOK
DELIGHT IN TANGLING HIS
MATES AND THE TRACES.

THEY QUARRELED
AND BICKERED MORE
THAN EVER AMONG
THEMSELVES.

ONE NIGHT NEAR A POLICE CAMP, DUB TURNED UP A *RABBIT,* BLUNDERED IT AND MISSED IT. FIFTY HUSKIES FROM THE CAMP JOINED THE TEAM AS THEY *CHASED* IT DOWNRIVER.

BUCK LED THE *PACK,* SIXTY STRONG, OLD *INSTINCTS* STIRRING HIS BLOOD. HE FELT THE HUNT, THE DESIRE TO KILL.

THERE IS AN *ECSTASY* THAT MARKS THE SUMMIT OF LIFE. IT COMES WHEN ONE IS MOST ALIVE. THE *ARTIST,* CAUGHT IN HIS CRAFT. THE *SOLDIER,* MAD ON THE BATTLEFIELD.

IT CAME TO BUCK, SOUNDING THE *WOLF-CRY,* STRAINING FOR THE PREY.

THE SURGING OF *LIFE...* THE JOY OF *MUSCLE,* SINEW AND JOINTS, TOGETHER IN ALL THAT WAS NOT DEATH.

BUT *DEATH* WAS PRESENT ON THE TUNDRA.

SPITZ, COLD AND CALCULATING, LEFT THE PACK AND CUT ACROSS WHERE THE CREEK MADE A *BEND* AROUND. HE LEAPT AND TOOK THE RABBIT.

THE RABBIT *SHRIEKED*, A CRY OF LIFE IN THE *GRIP* OF DEATH... AND THE PACK RAISED A *HOWL* OF DELIGHT AT BUCK'S HEELS.

BUCK DID NOT CRY OUT. HE *DROVE* INTO SPITZ, AND THEY ROLLED SLASHING, SHOULDER TO SHOULDER IN THE SNOW.

THE TIME HAD COME. IT WAS TO THE *DEATH.* ALL WAS CALM. THE DOGS DREW UP IN AN EXPECTANT CIRCLE, THEIR EYES GLEAMING AND THEIR BREATHS DRIFTING SLOWLY UPWARD.

TO BUCK IT WAS NOTHING NEW OR STRANGE, THIS SCENE OF OLD TIME.

IT WAS AS THOUGH IT HAD ALWAYS BEEN THE WONTED WAY OF THINGS.

SPITZ WAS A PRACTICED *FIGHTER.* WHERE BUCK'S FANGS STRUCK, HIS ENEMY'S COUNTERED THEM.

IN VAIN BUCK STROVE TO SINK HIS TEETH IN THE NECK OF THE BIG WHITE DOG, BUT WAS SLASHED DOWN EACH TIME.

THE FIGHT GREW *DESPERATE* AND BUCK GREW WINDED. THE CIRCLE EYED HIM, READY TO *FINISH* HIM OFF.

BUT BUCK HAD PROMISED NEVER TO GO *DOWN.*

HE *RUSHED,* AS THOUGH ATTEMPTING A SHOULDER ATTACK...

...BUT SWEPT LOW, *TEETH CLOSING* ON SPITZ'S FORE LEG.

BUCK REPEATED THE *TRICK,* BREAKING THE RIGHT LEG AND SPITZ STRUGGLED TO STAY UP.

HE SAW THE SILENT CIRCLE CLOSING IN UPON HIM AS HE HAD SEEN SIMILAR CIRCLES CLOSE IN UPON BEATEN ANTAGONISTS IN THE PAST. ONLY THIS TIME HE WAS THE ONE WHO WAS BEATEN.

THERE WAS NO HOPE FOR HIM. BUCK MOVED IN FOR THE *FINAL RUSH,* MERCY RESERVED FOR GENTLER CLIMES. SPITZ SNARLED, HOPING TO *FRIGHTEN OFF* IMPENDING DEATH.

THE DARK CIRCLE BECAME A DOT ON THE *MOON-FLOODED SNOW* AS SPITZ DISAPPEARED FROM VIEW. BUCK WATCHED, THE SUCCESSFUL *CHAMPION.*

THE DOMINANT *PRIMORDIAL BEAST* WHO HAD MADE HIS KILL...

...AND FOUND IT *GOOD.*

THE NEXT MORNING FRANCOIS DISCOVERED SPITZ MISSING AND BUCK COVERED WITH WOUNDS.

DAT BUCK *TWO* DEVILS,

BUCK FIGHT LIKE *TWO* HELLS.

DAT SPITZ *FIGHT* LIKE HELL.

NOW WE MAKE *GOOD TIME.* NO MORE TROUBLE.

THEY *LOADED* THE SLED AND FRANCOIS *HARNESSED* THE DOGS.

BUCK TROTTED TO THE *PLACE* SPITZ HAD OCCUPIED.

BUT FRANCOIS BROUGHT *SOLLEKS...*

...JUDGING HIM THE *BEST* LEAD DOG LEFT.

BUCK SPRANG UPON SOL-LEKS IN A
FURY, DRIVING HIM BACK AND STANDING
IN HIS PLACE. THE OLD DOG
RETREATED WITH FEAR.

FRANCOIS BECAME *ANGRY,* HEFTING
A HEAVY CLUB.

BUCK WAS *WISE* IN THE WAY OF CLUBS
AND RETREATED, SNARLING WITH
BITTERNESS.

FRANCOIS CALLED BUCK, READY TO
PUT HIM IN HIS *OLD PLACE* BY
DAVE. BUT BUCK WAS IN OPEN
REVOLT. HE HAD EARNED
LEADERSHIP. IT WAS HIS BY RIGHT.

HE WOULD NOT BE
CONTENT WITH LESS.

AFTER HOURS OF FIGHTING AND LOST TIME, FRANCOIS THREW DOWN HIS CLUB AND HARNESSED THE TRIUMPHANT BUCK.

BUCK TOOK THE REINS OF LEADERSHIP, AND SHOWED HIMSELF THE SUPERIOR OF SPITZ.

HE LICKED THE TEAM INTO SHAPE AND ONCE MORE, THE DOGS LEAPED AS ONE DOG IN THE TRACES.

BUT IT WAS IN GIVING THE LAW THAT BUCK EXCELLED.

NEVAIRE SUCH A DOG AS BUCK, *EH?*

HIM WORTH *ONE THOUSAND DOLLAR,* EH, PERRAULT?

PERRAULT AGREED. HE WAS AHEAD OF THE RECORD, AND GAINING DAY BY DAY.

WITH BUCK HANDING DOWN THE LAW, THEY COVERED THE THIRTY MILE RIVER IN *ONE DAY,* A TRIP THAT HAD TAKEN TEN COMING IN.

THEY DASHED FROM LAKE LE BARGE, HITTING THE NEXT SEVENTY MILES OF LAKE SO *FAST* THAT THE MAN RUNNING TOWED BEHIND AT THE END OF A ROPE.

IT WAS A *RECORD RUN*...FORTY MILES A DAY FOR FOURTEEN DAYS.

ON THE LAST NIGHT, THEY DROPPED DOWN THE SEA SLOPE, THE LIGHTS OF *SKAGUAY* BELOW.

FOR THREE DAYS THE TEAM WAS THE CENTER OF A *WORSHIPFUL CROWD* OF MUSHERS.

NEXT CAME OFFICAL ORDERS.

AND LIKE OTHER MEN, FRANCOIS AND PERRAULT *PASSED* FROM HIS LIFE FOR GOOD.

A SCOTCH HALF-BREED TOOK CHARGE OF THE *TEAM,* AND WITH A DOZEN OTHER SLEDS THEY STARTED BACK TO DAWSON.

IT WAS NO LIGHT RUNNING NOW, BUT HEAVY TOIL EACH DAY, FOR THIS WAS THE MAIL TRAIN, CARRYING WORD TO THE MEN WHO SOUGHT GOLD UNDER THE SHADOW OF THE POLE.

BUCK DID NOT LIKE IT BUT BORE UP WELL TO THE WORK, SEEING THAT HIS *MATES* DID THEIR SHARE.

EACH DAY LIKE THE NEXT. THEY BROKE IN THE MORNING AND MADE CAMP AT *NIGHT.*

THE TEAM WAS *FED* WITH THE OTHER FIVE-SCORE DOGS. THERE WERE *FIGHTERS* AMONG THEM, BUT THREE BATTLES BROUGHT BUCK TO MASTERY.

AT NIGHT, BUCK LOVED TO LIE BY THE FIRE, BLINKING DREAMILY AT THE FLAMES. SOMETIMES HE THOUGHT OF THE HOUSE IN SANTA CLARA.

BUT OFTENER HE REMEMBERED THE MAN IN THE SWEATER, CURLY'S DEATH, AND THE *FIGHT* WITH SPITZ.

MEMORIES AND *INSTINCTS* QUICKENED AND BECAME ALIVE AGAIN.

SOMETIMES THE *FLAMES* WERE OF ANOTHER FIRE...

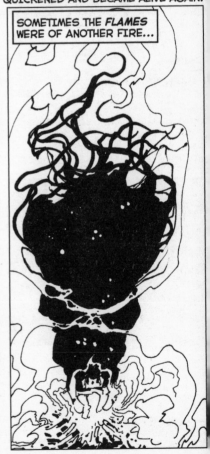

...AND THAT HE SAW ANOTHER MAN BEFORE HIM.

A *MAN* SQUAT AND HAIRY, UTTERING *SOUNDS* IN THE DARKNESS.

HE *CROUCHED*, CAT-LIKE, IN PERPETUAL FEAR OF THINGS SEEN AND UNSEEN.

HE SEEMED *AFRAID* OF THE DARKNESS INTO WHICH HE CONSTANTLY PEERED.

AS THE MAN SLEPT, BUCK SAW GLEAMING *COALS* IN THE DARKNESS.

THE EYES OF *GREAT BEASTS* OF PREY. HE COULD HEAR THE CRASHING OF THEIR BODIES THROUGH THE UNDERGROWTH IN THE NIGHT.

DREAMING BY THE YUKON BANK, THE SOUNDS OF *ANOTHER WORLD* MADE HIS HAIR RISE...

YOU, BUCK! *WAKE UP!*

...UNTIL SOMETHING BROUGHT HIM BACK TO *REALITY.*

IT WAS A HARD TRIP, WITH THE MAIL BEHIND THEM, AND *HEAVY WORK* WORE THEM DOWN.

THEY WERE IN *POOR CONDITION* UPON REACHING DAWSON AND SHOULD HAVE HAD TEN DAYS' REST.

BUT IN *TWO DAYS' TIME* THEY LEFT LOADED WITH LETTERS FOR THE OUTSIDE.

THE DOGS WERE *TIRED*, THE MEN GRUMBLING, AND CONSTANT SNOW CREATED A SOFTER, *DIFFICULT TRAIL*.

EACH NIGHT, THE *WEARY DOGS* WERE ATTENDED TO FIRST.

STILL, THEIR STRENGTH WENT DOWN.

BUCK STOOD IT, KEEPING HIS MATES TO THEIR WORK. BILLEE WHIMPERED AND JOE WAS *SOUR* AS EVER. SOLLEKS WAS *UNAPPROACHABLE,* BLIND SIDE OR NOT.

BUT IT WAS *DAVE* WHO SUFFERED MOST OF ALL.

SOMETHING HAD GONE WRONG WITH HIM. HE BECAME MORE MOROSE AND IRRITABLE.

SOMETIMES WHEN JERKED BY A SUDDEN *STOP* OR STRAINING TO START HE WOULD CRY IN PAIN.

THE DRIVER FOUND *NOTHING.* THE MEN COULD LOCATE NO BROKEN BONES OR THE *SOURCE* OF THE PROBLEM.

AT CASSIAR BAR, THE HALF-BREED *PULLED* HIM FROM THE TEAM, MAKING THE NEXT DOG FAST TO THE SLED. HE MEANT TO GIVE DAVE REST.

SICK AS HE WAS, DAVE COULD NOT BEAR THAT ANOTHER DOG SHOULD DO HIS WORK.

HE RAN *ALONGSIDE,* ATTACKING SOL-LEKS. HE FLOUNDERED IN THE SOFT SNOW TILL EXHAUSTED.

THEN HE FELL, AND LAY WHERE HE FELL. WITH THE LAST REMNANT OF STRENGTH, HE STAGGERED ALONG UNTIL THEY *STOPPED.* WHEN THE DRIVER RETURNED, *READY* TO GO ON...

...HE WAS SHOCKED TO FIND DAVE HAD BITTEN THROUGH SOL-LEKS'S TRACES, AND WAS STANDING IN HIS PROPER PLACE.

DAVE WAS *HARNESSED* IN AGAIN AND HE PULLED PROUDLY. SEVERAL TIMES HE *FELL* AND WAS *DRAGGED* IN THE TRACES.

BUT HE HELD OUT TILL CAMP WAS REACHED.

MORNING FOUND HIM *TOO WEAK* TO TRAVEL. AT HARNESS-UP TIME, HE TRIED TO *CRAWL* TO HIS DRIVER. HIS *STRENGTH* LEFT HIM AND THE *LAST* THEY SAW HIM HE LAY IN THE *SNOW,* YEARNING TO GO ON.

THEY COULD HEAR HIM MOURNFULLY *HOWLING.*

THE TRAIN WAS *HALTED.* THE SCOTCH HALF-BREED RETRACED HIS STEPS.

THE MAN CAME BACK. THE WHIPS SNAPPED, THE SLEDS CHURNED ALONG. BUT BUCK *KNEW,* AND EVERY DOG KNEW, WHAT HAD TAKEN PLACE BEHIND THE BELT OF RIVER TREES.

K-POW

THIRTY DAYS FROM DAWSON, THE DOGS PULLED INTO *SKAGUAY*, WORN OUT AND WORN DOWN.

HAVING COVERED HUNDREDS OF MILES WITH *TWO DAYS REST*, THE DRIVERS CONFIDENTLY EXPECTED A LONG STOPOVER.

BUT FRESH DOGS REPLACED THOSE WORTHLESS FOR THE TRAIL. AND AS WORTHLESS DOGS WERE TO BE GOTTEN RID OF, THE TEAM WAS SOLD.

THEY WERE *BOUGHT* BY TWO MEN FROM THE STATES: HAL AND CHARLES. BOTH WERE *OUT OF PLACE* IN THE NORTH.

THEIR CAMP WAS SLIPSHOD AND SLOVENLY, CARED FOR BY A *WOMAN* NAMED MERCEDES, HAL'S SISTER AND CHARLES'S WIFE.

BUCK WATCHED WITH *APPREHENSION* AS THEY HAPHAZARDLY LOADED THE SLED.

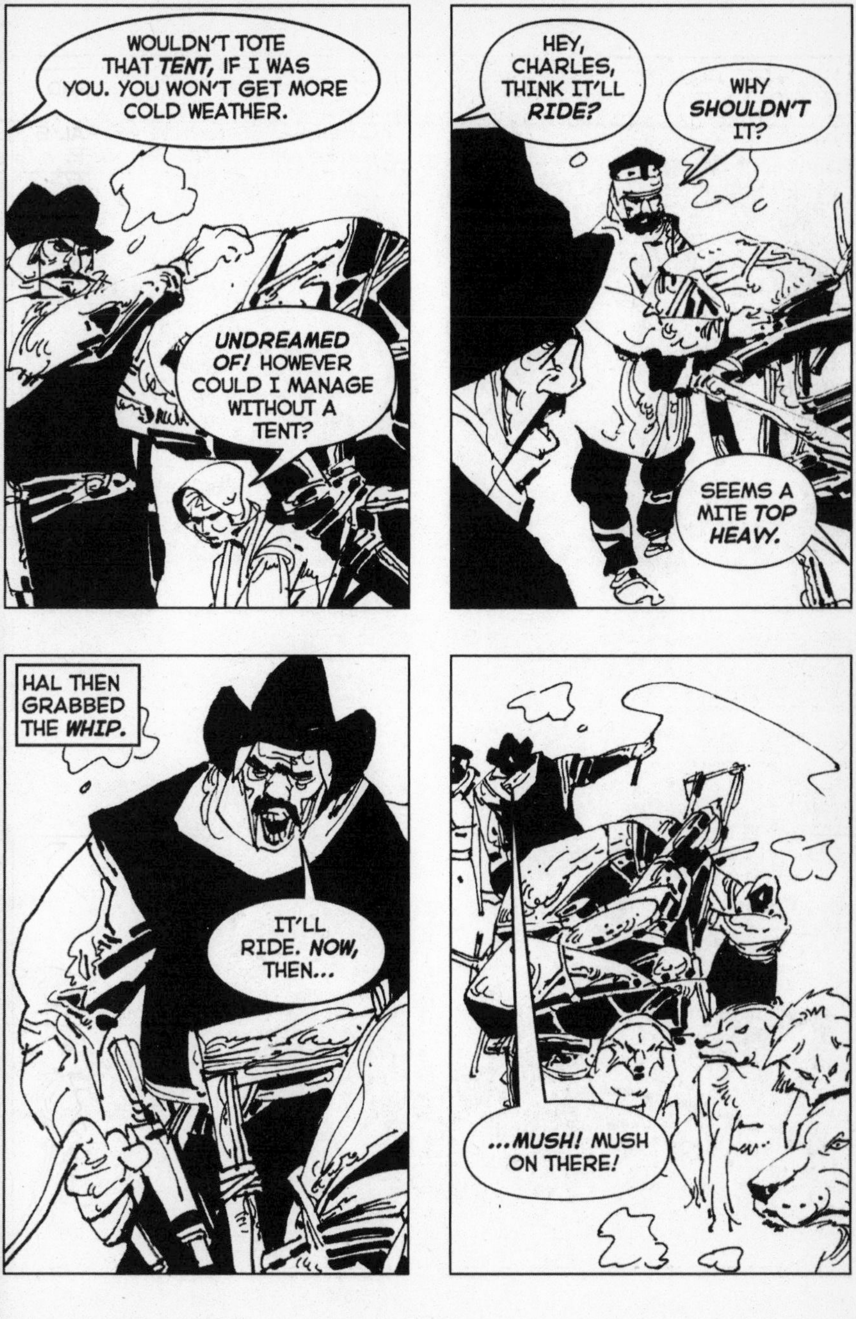
WOULDN'T TOTE THAT *TENT,* IF I WAS YOU. YOU WON'T GET MORE COLD WEATHER.
UNDREAMED OF! HOWEVER COULD I MANAGE WITHOUT A TENT?
HEY, CHARLES, THINK IT'LL *RIDE?*
WHY *SHOULDN'T* IT?
SEEMS A MITE *TOP HEAVY.*
HAL THEN GRABBED THE *WHIP.*
IT'LL RIDE. *NOW,* THEN...
...MUSH! MUSH ON THERE!

THE DOGS *STRAINED HARD* FOR A FEW MOMENTS, THEN RELAXED. THEY WERE UNABLE TO *MOVE* THE SLED.

LAZY BRUTES!

I'LL *SHOW* THEM!

YOU MUSTN'T!

YOU'VE GOT TO *WHIP* THEM TO GET ANYTHING FROM THEM!

IT'S *THEIR* WAY! ASK THOSE MEN!

THEY'RE *WEAK.*

THEY NEED A *REST.*

HAL'S WHIP AGAIN FELL ON THE DOGS.

FOR THE DOGS' SAKE, YOU CAN HELP BY BREAKIN' OUT THAT SLED.

THE RUNNERS ARE FROZE FAST.

ANOTHER ATTEMPT WAS MADE. HAL BROKE OUT THE RUNNERS. THE UNWIELDY SLED FORGED ON.

BRAKKK

THE DOGS *STRUGGLED* DOWN THE PATH, WHERE IT SLOPED INTO THE MAIN ROAD. IT WOULD HAVE REQUIRED AN EXPERIENCED MAN TO KEEP THE TOP-HEAVY SLED UPRIGHT. HAL WAS NOT SUCH A MAN. THEN...

KRASH

THE DOGS NEVER STOPPED, RAGING FROM THE *ILL TREATMENT* AND UNJUST LOAD.

STOP!

BUCK BROKE INTO A RUN, THE TEAM FOLLOWING HIS LEAD. THE DOGS DASHED ON UP THE STREET, ADDING TO THE GAIETY OF *SKAGUAY* AS THEY SCATTERED THE REMAINDER OF THE OUTFIT ALONG ITS CHIEF THOROUGHFARE.

GET *BACK* HERE!

THEY OVERHAULED AND, TO MERCEDES'S *DISMAY*, REMOVED EXTRA WEIGHT. THEY ADDED *SIX OUTSIDE DOGS*, BRINGING THEM TO FOURTEEN.

THE NEW DOGS DID NOT SEEM TO KNOW ANYTHING AND BUCK'S TEAM LOOKED AT THEM WITH *DISGUST*.

KIND-HEARTED *CITIZENS* COLLECTED THE DOGS AND GOODS, OFFERING *ADVICE* ON HOW BEST TO PACK.

THEY DID NOT TAKE KINDLY TO TRACE AND *TRAIL*, AND BUCK COULD NOT TEACH THEM.

AND *WORSE*, THE MEN DID NOT REALIZE ONE SLED COULD NOT CARRY *FOOD* FOR FOURTEEN DOGS.

LATE NEXT *MORNING* BUCK LED THEM OUT.

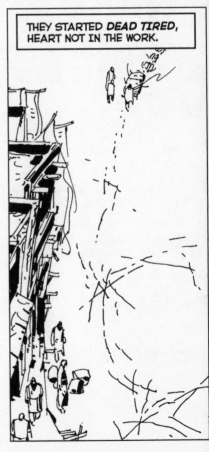

THEY STARTED *DEAD TIRED*, HEART NOT IN THE WORK.

BUCK COULD NOT *DEPEND* ON THE MEN OR THE WOMAN. IT WAS PLAIN THAT THEY DID NOT KNOW ANYTHING, NOR COULD THEY LEARN.

IT TOOK HALF THE NIGHT TO *PITCH A SLOVENLY CAMP* AND HALF THE MORNING TO LOAD.

SOME DAYS THEY DID NOT MAKE *TEN MILES*. OTHERS THEY WERE UNABLE TO START AT ALL.

HAL *OVERFED* THEM.

INEVITABLY, THEY WENT SHORT ON *FOOD*. BUT IT WAS NOT FOOD THE DOGS NEEDED, BUT REST.

HALF THE FOOD WAS GONE, BUT NOT HALF THE *DISTANCE*. SO HAL BEGAN TO UNDERFEED.

IT WAS SIMPLE TO GIVE DOGS *LESS FOOD*, BUT IMPOSSIBLE TO MAKE THEM TRAVEL FASTER.

THE **FIRST** TO GO WAS DUB.

HIS WRENCHED SHOULDER WENT UN**TREATED** AND HAL SHOT HIM.

THE **OUTSIDE DOGS** SOON FOLLOWED, UNABLE TO SURVIVE ON HALF A HUSKY'S RATION.

BY THIS TIME ALL AMENITIES AND GENTLENESS OF THE SOUTHLAND HAD FALLEN AWAY FROM THE THREE PEOPLE. SHORN OF ITS GLAMOUR AND ROMANCE, ARCTIC TRAVEL BECAME TO THEM A REALITY TOO HARSH.

THEY WERE NEVER TOO WEARY TO *ARGUE.*

CHARLES AND HAL *WRANGLED,* MERCEDES PLAYING ENDS AGAINST THE MIDDLE.

IT WAS AN UNENDING *FAMILY QUARREL,* RANGING FROM THE DIVISION OF WORK TO DIFFERING VIEWS ON ART.

IN THE MEANTIME, THE FIRE WAS *UNBUILT* AND THE DOGS UNFED.

AND THERE WAS MERCEDES.

SHE RODE FOR DAYS, *DRAGGED* BY THE WEAK DOGS. ONCE, THE MEN TOOK HER OFF BY FORCE AND SHE *SAT* ON THE TRAIL LIKE A CHILD.

AFTER THREE MILES, THEY *UNLOADED* AND RETURNED FOR HER.

THE DOGS WERE WALKING *SKELETONS*, NUMB TO PAIN, DULL AND DISTANT.

AND THROUGH IT ALL, BUCK STAGGERED ALONG AT THE HEAD.

THERE CAME A DAY WHEN BILLEE *FELL* AND COULD NOT RISE.

HAL TOOK THE AXE AND KNOCKED HIM ON THE HEAD AS HE LAY, THEN CUT HIS BODY FROM THE HARNESS. THE NEXT DAY, KOONA WENT.

FIVE *REMAINED:* JOE, PIKE, SOL-LEKS, TEEK AND BUCK, ALL NEAR *BLIND* WITH WEAKNESS.

DEATH WAS VERY CLOSE TO THEM. AND STILL THEY TRUDGED ON.

IT WAS BEAUTIFUL *SPRING WEATHER,* BUT NEITHER DOGS NOR HUMAN WERE AWARE.

THE GHOSTLY WINTER *SILENCE* HAD GIVEN TO THE GREAT SPRING MURMUR. THE WHOLE DAY WAS A BLAZE OF SUNSHINE.

THE *YUKON* STRAINED TO BREAK THE *ICE* THAT BOUND IT DOWN.

THE MURMUR AROSE FROM ALL THE LANDS FRAUGHT WITH THE JOY OF LIVING.

AND AMID THIS RENEWAL OF *LIFE,* LIKE WAYFARERS TO *DEATH,* WALKED THE TWO MEN, THE WOMAN AND THE HUSKIES.

IN THIS MANNER, THEY STAGGERED INTO *JOHN THORNTON'S CAMP* AT WHITE RIVER.

THEY SAID THE *BOTTOM* WAS DROPPIN' OUT OF THE *TRAIL.*

THEY TOLD US WE'D NEVER MAKE *WHITE RIVER* AND HERE WE ARE.

MY NAME'S *HAL.*

JOHN THORNTON. THEY TOLD YOU *TRUE.*

I WOULDN'T *RISK* MY HIDE ON THAT ICE FOR ALL THE *GOLD* IN ALASKA.

ALL THE SAME, WE'LL GO ON TO *DAWSON.*

SUIT YERSELF.

HYAH! GET UP THERE, BUCK! MUSH ON!

GET UP THERE!

THE TEAM DID NOT *RISE* AND HAL'S *WHIP* FLASHED MERCILESSLY. JOHN THORNTON HELD HIS TONGUE AND *WATCHED.*

THORNTON WENT ON WHITTLING. IT WAS IDLE, HE KNEW, TO GET BETWEEN A FOOL AND HIS FOLLY.

SOL-LEKS WAS THE *FIRST* TO RISE, FOLLOWED BY TEEK AND JOE.

PIKE MADE PAINFUL EFFORTS. TWICE HE FELL OVER, ON THE THIRD ATTEMPT HE MANAGED TO RISE. BUCK MADE NO EFFORT. HE HAD MADE UP HIS MIND NOT TO GET UP.

THE LASH BIT INTO HIM AGAIN AND AGAIN, BUT HE NEITHER WHINED NOR STRUGGLED.

THORNTON BEGAN TO *SPEAK*, THEN CHANGED HIS MIND. *MOISTURE* FILLED HIS EYES.

HAL EXHCANGED THE WHIP FOR THE CUSTOMARY CLUB.

BUCK REFUSED TO MOVE UNDER THE RAIN OF HEAVIER BLOWS.

HE *REFUSED* TO STIR. SO MUCH HAD HE *SUFFERED* THAT THE BLOWS DID NOT HURT. AND AS THEY CONTINUED TO FALL UPON HIM, THE SPARK OF LIFE WITHIN FLICKERED AND WENT DOWN. HE NO LONGER FELT ANYTHING.

SUDDENLY, WITH A STRANGLED *CRY*, JOHN THORNTON *SPRANG* FORWARD AND KNOCKED HAL FROM HIS FEET.

LEAVE HIM *BE!*

IF YOU STRIKE THAT DOG AGAIN, I'LL *KILL* YOU.

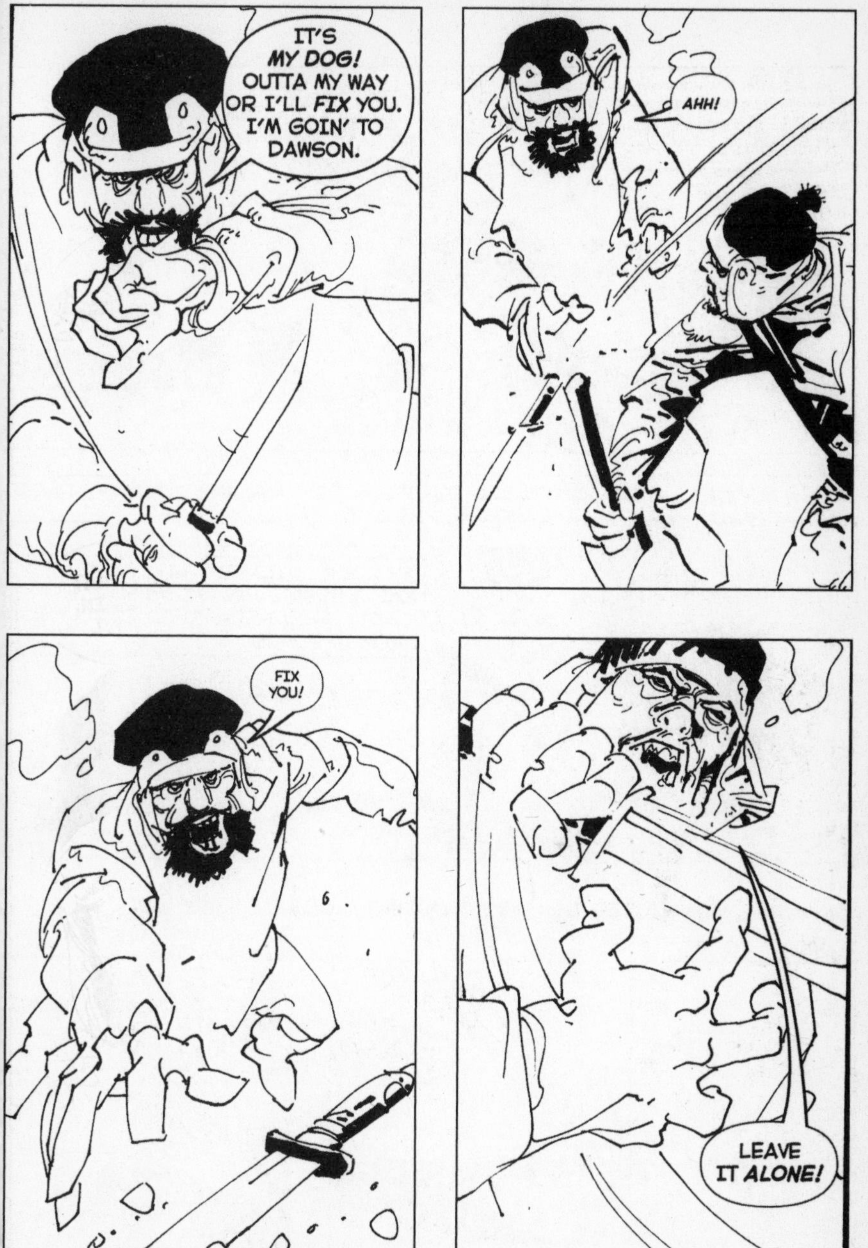
IT'S
MY DOG!
OUTTA MY WAY
OR I'LL FIX YOU.
I'M GOIN' TO
DAWSON.
AHH!
FIX
YOU!
LEAVE
IT ALONE!

HAL HAD NO *FIGHT* LEFT IN HIM AND BUCK WAS TOO NEAR *DEAD* TO BE OF USE.

A FEW MINUTES LATER THEY PULLED OUT FROM THE BANK AND DOWN THE RIVER. BUCK HEARD THEM GO AND RAISED HIS HEAD TO SEE.

AS BUCK WATCHED THEM, THORNTON KNELT BESIDE HIM AND WITH ROUGH, KINDLY HANDS SEARCHED FOR BROKEN BONES.

DOG AND MAN WATCHED THE SLED CRAWLING ALONG OVER THE ICE.

THE SLED WAS A QUARTER MILE AWAY WHEN A WHOLE SECTION OF ICE GAVE WAY.

DOGS AND HUMANS DISAPPEARED, *SCREAMS* RINGING ACROSS THE RIVER. A YAWNING HOLE WAS ALL THAT WAS TO BE SEEN.

THE *BOTTOM* HAD DROPPED OUT OF THE TRAIL.

YOU POOR DEVIL.

JOHN THORNTON HAD FROZE HIS FEET IN THE PREVIOUS WINTER, HIS PARTNERS LEFT HIM TO GET WELL.

LYING BY THE RIVER, BUCK WON BACK HIS *STRENGTH.*

WITH *SKEET* AND *NIG,* A SETTER AND HOUND, HE WAITED FOR JOHN'S PARTNERS TO RETURN AND *FERRY* THEM TO DAWSON.

THEY SHARED IN THORNTON'S *KINDLINESS* AND AS BUCK ROMPED TO HEALTH, HE FOUND GENUINE *LOVE* FOR THE FIRST TIME.

THE *IDEAL MASTER,* JOHN THORNTON SAW TO THEIR WELFARE AS IF THEY WERE HIS CHILDREN.

BUCK KNEW NO GREATER *JOY* THAN JOHN'S EMBRACE.

SUCH WAS THE COMMUNION IN WHICH THEY LIVED, THE STRENGTH OF BUCK'S GAZE WOULD DRAW JOHN THORNTON'S HEAD AROUND, AND HE WOULD RETURN THE GAZE.

GOD, YOU CAN ALL BUT *SPEAK.*

WHILE HE WENT WILD WITH HAPPINESS WHEN THORNTON TOUCHED HIM OR SPOKE TO HIM, BUCK DID NOT SEEK THESE TOKENS. BUCK WAS CONTENT TO ADORE AT A DISTANCE.

AND SO THEY LIVED, *HEARTS* SHINING IN THEIR EYES.

BUCK DID NOT LET THORNTON FROM HIS *SIGHT*, AFRAID HE WOULD PASS FROM HIS LIFE AS OTHERS HAD.

BUT IN SPITE OF THIS GREAT LOVE HE BORE THORNTON, THE STRAIN OF THE *PRIMITIVE* REMAINED ALIVE AND ACTIVE.

HE WAS A THING OF THE *WILD*, COME TO SIT BY JOHN THORNTON'S *FIRE*, RATHER THAN A DOG OF THE SOUTHLAND STAMPED WITH MARKS OF CIVILIZATION.

THE SHADES OF *CANINES PAST* PROMPTED
HIM TO RUN, HUNT, AND KILL.

EACH DAY THE *CLAIMS* OF MANKIND SLIPPED FARTHER AWAY...

...A *CALL* SOUNDING TO HIM FROM THE FOREST.

BUT THE *LOVE* FOR JOHN THORNTON DREW HIM *BACK.*

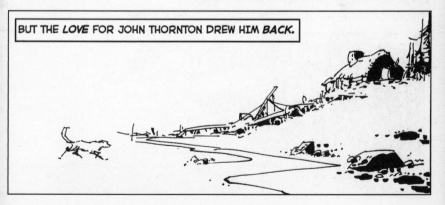

THORNTON ALONE *HELD* HIM. WHEN HIS PARTNERS, HANS AND PETE, ARRIVED BUCK SIMPLY *TOLERATED* THEM.

FOR THORNTON, HOWEVER, BUCK'S LOVE SEEMED TO GROW AND GROW. NOTHING WAS TOO GREAT TO DO, WHEN THORNTON COMMANDED.

ONE DAY, A THOUGHTLESS WHIM SEIZED THORNTON.

JUMP, BUCK!

WAIT! BUCK, NO!

IT'S *UNCANNY!*

NO, IT'S SPLENDID AND *TERRIBLE.* IT MAKES ME AFRAID.

I'M NOT HANKERING TO BE THE MAN THAT LAYS HANDS ON YOU WHILE HE'S AROUND.

AT *CIRCLE CITY,* PETE'S APPREHENSIONS WERE REALIZED WHEN THORNTON TRIED TO STOP A *QUARREL* BETWEEN A TENDERFOOT AND "BLACK" BURTON.

BURTON **STRUCK** OUT WITHOUT WARNING.

THORNTON WAS SENT SPINNING.

THOSE WHO WERE LOOKING ON HEARD WHAT WAS NEITHER BARK NOR YELP, BUT A SOMETHING LIKE A ROAR. THEY SAW BUCK'S BODY RISE UP IN THE AIR AS HE LEFT THE FLOOR FOR BURTON'S THROAT.

BUCK WAS FORCED **BACK** BY CLUBS, AS A SURGEON CHECKED BURTON.

A "**MINERS MEETING**" DISCHARGED BUCK, WHO HAD SUFFICIENT **PROVOCATION**, AND HIS **REPUTATION** WAS MADE.

HIS NAME SPREAD THROUGH EVERY CAMP IN ALASKA.

THAT FALL, BUCK *SAVED* THORNTON'S LIFE AGAIN ON THE *FORTY MILE CREEK.* AS THEY LINED A *BOAT* DOWN A STRETCH OF *RAPIDS,* THORNTON FELL OUT AND WAS CARRIED DOWNSTREAM.

PETE AND HANS ATTACHED A LINE TO BUCK'S NECK AND SHOULDERS. HANS PAID OUT THE ROPE. PETE KEPT CLEAR OF THE COILS.

THORNTON SAW HIM COMING.

BUCK *STRUCK* HIM, AND THORNTON CLOSED BOTH *ARMS* AROUND HIS SHAGGY NECK.

STRANGLING AND *HALF-DROWNED*, THEY CAME TO THE *BANK* WHERE THORNTON, GOING OVER BUCK'S BODY, FOUND *THREE BROKEN RIBS.*

THAT SETTLES IT. WE CAMP RIGHT HERE.

AND CAMP THEY DID, TILL BUCK'S RIBS KNITTED AND HE WAS ABLE TO TRAVEL.

THAT WINTER, AT DAWSON, BUCK PERFORMED ANOTHER EXPLOIT THAT PUT HIS NAME MANY NOTCHES HIGHER ON THE TOTEM POLE OF ALASKAN FAME.

IT WAS BROUGHT ABOUT BY A CONVERSATION IN THE ELDORADO SALOON, IN WHICH MEN WAXED BOASTFUL OF THEIR FAVORITE DOGS.

A MAN NAMED *MATTHEWSON* CLAIMED HIS DOG COULD START A SLED WITH *SEVEN HUNDRED POUNDS* AND WALK OFF.

BUCK CAN START A *THOUSAND!*

BREAKING IT OUT AND *WALKING* A HUNDRED YARDS?

105

I'VE GOT A THOUSAND DOLLARS IN *GOLD* SAYS HE CAN'T.

AND I'VE A *SLED* OUTSIDE WITH TWENTY FIFTY-POUND SACKS OF FLOUR ON IT.

THORNTON'S *BLUFF* HAD BEEN CALLED. HE DID NOT KNOW WHETHER BUCK COULD START A THOUSAND POUNDS. HALF A TON*!*

HE *BORROWED* A THOUSAND AND THE SALOON EMPTIED INTO THE STREET.

THE SLED HAD *FROZEN FAST* AND MEN OFFERED ODDS OF TWO TO ONE THAT BUCK COULD *NOT BUDGE* IT.

MATTHEWSON INSISTED "BREAK IT OUT" MEANT BREAKING THE RUNNERS FROM THE FROZEN GRIP OF THE SNOW. A MAJORITY OF THE MEN WHO HAD WITNESSED THE MAKING OF THE BET DECIDED IN HIS FAVOR.

ODDS WENT UP THREE TO ONE AGAINST BUCK. THERE WERE NO TAKERS. NOT A MAN BELIEVED HIM CAPABLE OF THE FEAT.

107

THREE TO ONE? I'LL LAY YOU *ANOTHER THOUSAND* AT THAT FIGURE, THORNTON! WHAT DO YOU SAY?

THORNTON'S DOUBT WAS STRONG IN HIS FACE, BUT HIS FIGHTING *SPIRIT* WAS AROUSED.

TOGETHER WITH PETE AND HANS, HE *POOLED* ANOTHER TWO HUNDRED. BUCK FELT THAT HE MUST DO A *GREAT THING* FOR JOHN THORNTON.

THE MEN ADMIRED BUCK'S *CONDITION* AND THE ODDS WENT DOWN.

GAD' I OFFER *EIGHT HUNDRED* FOR YOUR DOG, JUST AS HE STANDS.

YOU MUST *STAND OFF* FROM HIM. FREE PLAY AND PLENTY OF *ROOM!*

THE CROWD FELL SILENT. THORNTON KNELT DOWN BY BUCK'S SIDE.

HE DID NOT PLAYFULLY SHAKE HIM, AS WAS HIS WONT, OR MURMUR SOFT LOVE CURSES. BUT HE WHISPERED IN BUCK'S EAR...

AS YOU LOVE ME BUCK.

AS YOU LOVE ME.

NOW, BUCK.

BUCK SWUNG TO THE RIGHT, THE TRACES AND HIS MUSCLES GOING TAUT WITH HIS STRAIN.

GEE!

THE SLED *SWAYED*, THEN TREMBLED.

KKKRRAKKR

HAW!

NOW, MUSH!

THE SLED HALF-STARTED FORWARD.

THEN IT *LURCHED* AHEAD...

...AN INCH.

TWO INCHES.

MEN *GASPED* AND BEGAN TO BREATHE, UNAWARE THAT THEY HAD STOPPED.

AS BUCK NEARED THE END OF THE HUNDRED YARDS, A *CHEER* BEGAN TO GROW.

IT BURST TO A *ROAR* AS HE PASSED THE *MARKER* AND HALTED ON COMMAND.

THORNTON FELL ON HIS *KNEES* BESIDE BUCK...SHAKING HIM BACK AND FORTH, SOFTLY AND LOVINGLY.

GAD, SIR! I'LL GIVE A *THOUSAND* FOR HIM!

TWELVE HUNDRED, SIR!

NO, SIR.

YOU CAN GO TO *HELL*, SIR.

THE *MONEY* BUCK WON ALLOWED THORNTON TO PAY OFF *DEBTS* AND JOURNEY EAST WITH HIS PARTNERS.

WITH HALF A DOZEN DOGS, THEY SEARCHED FOR A FABLED LOST MINE. MANY MEN HAD SOUGHT IT; FEW HAD FOUND IT. AND MORE THAN A FEW THERE WERE WHO HAD NEVER RETURNED FROM THE QUEST.

THIS LOST MINE WAS STEEPED IN TRAGEDY AND SHROUDED IN MYSTERY.

TWO MONTHS THEY *SEARCHED,* ACROSS SUMMER AND WINTER. THEY WANDERED ON THE *TRAILS* OF MEN WHO HAD GONE BEFORE.

TO BUCK IT WAS BOUNDLESS DELIGHT, THIS HUNTING AND FISHING, AND INDEFINITE WANDERING THROUGH STRANGE PLACES.

AT THE END OF ALL THEIR WANDERING THEY FOUND A PLACE WHERE GOLD SHOWED LIKE YELLOW BUTTER ACROSS THE BOTTOM OF THE WASHING PAN.

THEY SOUGHT NO FARTHER. EACH DAY THEY WORKED EARNED THEM THOUSANDS OF DOLLARS IN CLEAN DUST AND NUGGETS. AND THEY WORKED EVERY DAY.

THERE WAS NOTHING FOR THE DOGS TO DO, SAVE THE HAULING IN OF MEAT NOW AND AGAIN THAT THORNTON KILLED.

BUCK SPENT HOURS MUSING BY THE FIRE. THE VISION OF THE SHORT-LEGGED HAIRY MAN CAME TO HIM MORE FREQUENTLY NOW.

BUCK WANDERED WITH HIM IN THAT OTHER WORLD WHICH HE REMEMBERED.

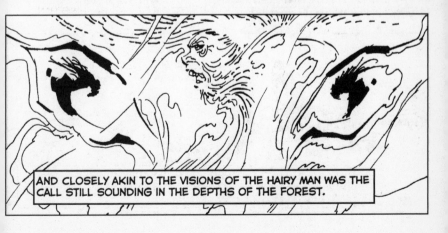

AND CLOSELY AKIN TO THE VISIONS OF THE HAIRY MAN WAS THE CALL STILL SOUNDING IN THE DEPTHS OF THE FOREST.

115

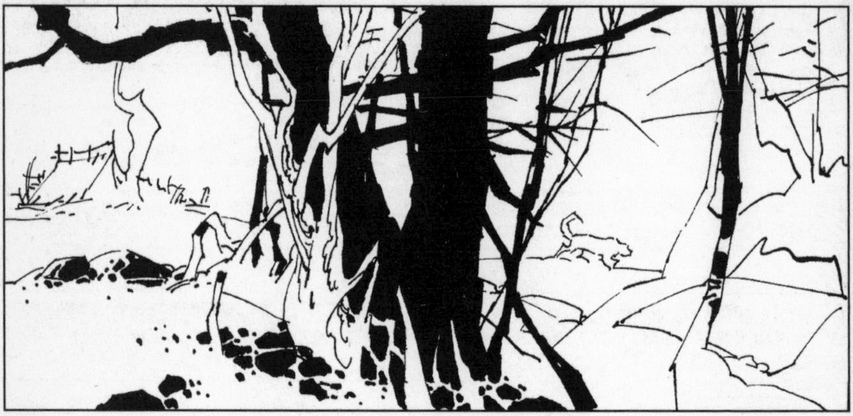

IT FILLED HIM WITH A GREAT UNREST AND STRANGE DESIRES. HE PURSUED THE CALL INTO THE FOREST, LOOKING FOR IT AS THOUGH IT WERE A TANGIBLE THING, BARKING SOFTLY OR DEFIANTLY, AS THE MOOD MIGHT DICTATE.

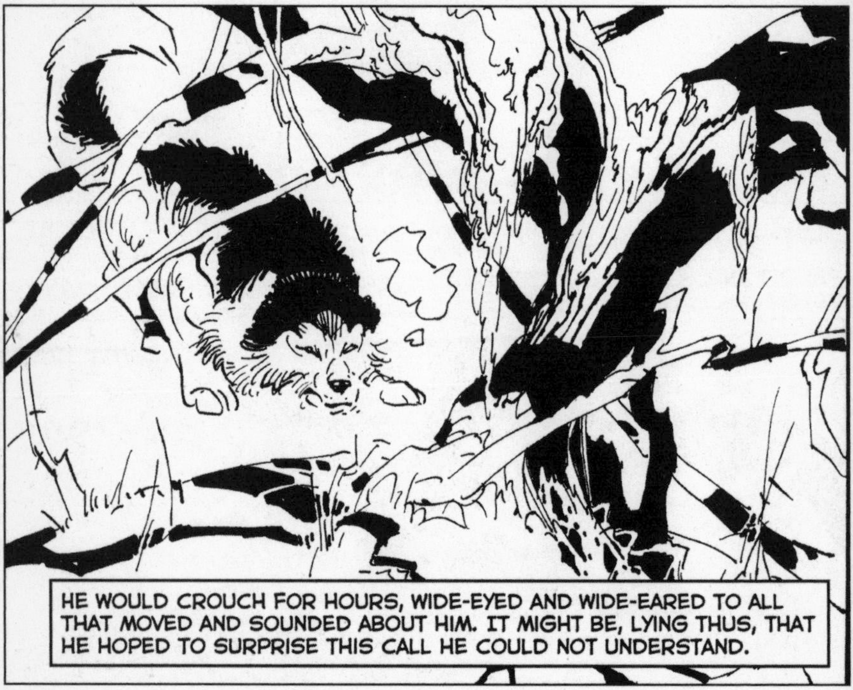
HE WOULD CROUCH FOR HOURS, WIDE-EYED AND WIDE-EARED TO ALL THAT MOVED AND SOUNDED ABOUT HIM. IT MIGHT BE, LYING THUS, THAT HE HOPED TO SURPRISE THIS CALL HE COULD NOT UNDERSTAND.

IRRESISTIBLE IMPULSES SEIZED HIM.

HE WOULD BE LYING IN CAMP, DOZING LAZILY IN THE HEAT OF THE DAY, WHEN SUDDENLY HIS HEAD WOULD LIFT AND HIS EARS COCK UP, AND HE WOULD SPRING TO HIS FEET AND DASH AWAY.

HE LOVED TO RUN DOWN DRY WATERCOURSES, AND TO CREEP AND SPY UPON THE BIRD LIFE IN THE WOODS.

BUT ESPECIALLY HE LOVED TO RUN IN THE DIM *TWILIGHT,* LISTENING TO THE FOREST AND SEEKING THE *MYSTERIOUS THING* THAT CALLED FOR HIM TO COME.

ONE NIGHT HE WOKE TO THE CLEAR SOUND OF THE *CALL*... A DRAWN OUT HOWL.

AROOOOO!

HE DREW *CLOSER* TO THE CRY, CAUTION IN EVERY MOVEMENT.

AROOOOO!

HE CAME TO AN *OPEN PLACE* AMONG THE TREES, AND THE *SOURCE* OF THE CRY: A LONG, LEAN TIMBER WOLF.

ARRROOOOO!

118

BUCK *APPROACHED,* EVERY MOVEMENT AN OVERTURE OF *FRIENDLINESS,* BUT THE WOLF FLED.

THEY *RAN,* AND BUCK DID NOT *ATTACK* BUT CIRCLED ABOUT HIM AND HEDGED HIM IN WITH FRIENDLY ADVANCES.

THE WOLF WAS *SUSPICIOUS* AND AFRAID, FOR BUCK WAS LARGER.

TIME AND AGAIN THEY *DANCED.* AND THE WOLF, SEEING NO HARM WAS INTENDED, *GREETED* BUCK.

THEY RAN THROUGH THE *TWILIGHT,* HOUR AFTER HOUR UNTIL SUNRISE.

BUCK WAS WILDLY GLAD. HE KNEW HE WAS AT LAST *ANSWERING* THE CALL, RUNNING BY THE SIDE OF HIS *WOOD BROTHER* TOWARD THE PLACE FROM WHERE THE CALL SURELY CAME.

THEY STOPPED BY A RUNNING *STREAM* TO DRINK...

...AND BUCK *REMEMBERED.*

BUCK STARTED BACK AND THE WILD BROTHER *RAN BY HIS SIDE WHINING SOFTLY.*

THEN HE SAT DOWN, POINTED HIS NOSE UPWARD AND HOWLED. IT WAS A MOURNFUL HOWL, AND AS BUCK HELD STEADILY ON HIS WAY HE HEARD IT GROW FAINTER UNTIL IT WAS LOST IN THE DISTANCE.

AROOOOO!

JOHN THORNTON WAS EATING DINNER WHEN BUCK DASHED INTO *CAMP* AND SPRANG UPON HIM IN A FRENZY OF AFFECTION.

FOR TWO DAYS AND NIGHTS BUCK NEVER LEFT CAMP, NEVER LET THORNTON OUT OF HIS SIGHT.

BUT AFTER TWO DAYS THE CALL IN THE FOREST BEGAN TO SOUND MORE IMPERIOUSLY THAN EVER.

HE WAS *HAUNTED* BY RECOLLECTIONS OF THE WILD BROTHER AND THE RUN THROUGH THE FOREST.

ONCE AGAIN HE TOOK TO WANDERING IN THE WOODS BUT THE WILD BROTHER CAME NO MORE.

AND THOUGH HE LISTENED THROUGH LONG VIGILS THE *MOURNFUL HOWL* WAS NEVER RAISED.

HE BEGAN TO STAY AWAY FROM CAMP FOR DAYS AT A TIME.

ONCE HE CROSSED THE DIVIDE AT THE HEAD OF THE CREEK. THERE HE WANDERED FOR A WEEK, SEEKING VAINLY FOR FRESH SIGNS OF THE WILD BROTHER.

BY THIS STREAM HE *KILLED* A LARGE BLACK BEAR, THE FIGHT AROUSING THE *LAST* LATENT REMNANTS OF HIS FEROCITY.

TWO DAYS LATER, WHEN HE RETURNED TO HIS KILL HE FOUND A DOZEN *WOLVERINES* FIGHTING OVER THE SPOIL. HE SCATTERED THEM LIKE CHAFF.

THE BLOOD-LONGING BECAME STRONGER THAN EVER BEFORE. HE WAS A THING THAT PREYED, SURVIVING IN A HOSTILE ENVIRONMENT WHERE ONLY THE STRONG SURVIVED. HE BECAME POSSESSED OF GREAT PRIDE IN HIMSELF.

BUT FOR HIS MUZZLE AND THE WHITE OF HIS CHEST HE MIGHT HAVE BEEN A *WOLF,* THE LARGEST OF THE BREED.

CUNNING, INTELLIGENT; VIRILE AND *DANGEROUS,* HE HAD BECOME A THING OF THE WILD.

HE WISHED STRONGLY FOR LARGER AND MORE FORMIDABLE QUARRY.

AND HE CAME UPON IT ONE DAY ON THE DIVIDE AT THE HEAD OF THE CREEK, A BANK OF TWENTY MOOSE.

ITS LEADER, A *GREAT BULL*, WAS SAVAGE AND WOUNDED...PERFECT PREY FOR BUCK.

BUCK PROCEEDED TO CUT IT FROM THE *HERD*, PATIENTLY ATTACKING, RETREATING AND THEN RETURNING ONCE MORE.

HE ATTACKED FROM ALL SIDES, WEARING OUT THE PATIENCE OF CREATURES PREYED UPON.

AS *TWILIGHT* FELL THE OLD BULL STOOD WITH LOWERED HEAD, WATCHING HIS MATES AS THEY SHAMBLED ON AT A RAPID PACE THROUGH THE FADING LIGHT. HE COULD NOT FOLLOW.

FROM THEN ON, BUCK NEVER LEFT HIS PREY.

NEVER GAVE IT A MOMENT'S REST.

THE GREAT HORNS *DROOPED* AND THE SHAMBLING TROT GREW WEAKER AND WEAKER.

AT THE END OF THE *FOURTH DAY,* HE PULLED THE GREAT MOOSE DOWN.

FOR A DAY AND NIGHT HE *REMAINED* BY THE KILL, EATING AND SLEEPING.

THEN HE TURNED HIS FACE TOWARDS *CAMP* AND JOHN THORNTON.

HE BROKE INTO THE LONG EASY LOPE, HOUR AFTER HOUR, NEVER AT A LOSS FOR THE TANGLED WAY.

AS HE HELD ON HE BECAME MORE AND MORE CONSCIOUS OF THE NEW STIR IN THE LAND. HE WAS OPPRESSED WITH A SENSE OF CALAMITY HAPPENING.

THREE MILES AWAY FROM CAMP HE CAME UPON A FRESH TRAIL THAT SENT HIS NECK HAIR RIPPLING AND BRISTLING. BUCK HURRIED ON, ALERT TO THE MULTITUDINOUS DETAILS WHICH TOLD A STORY--ALL BUT THE END.

HE REMARKED THE PREGNANT SILENCE OF THE FOREST.

AS BUCK SLID ALONG WITH THE OBSCURENESS OF A GLIDING SHADOW, HIS NOSE WAS JERKED TO THE SIDE AS THOUGH A POSITIVE FORCE HAD GRIPPED AND PULLED IT.

HE FOLLOWED A *SCENT*...

...AND FOUND *NIG*.

HE CAME UPON ONE OF THE SLED DOGS, THRASHING IN A *DEATH STRUGGLE.*

BUCK PASSED WITHOUT STOPPING.

FROM THE CAMP CAME THE FAINT SOUND OF MANY VOICES, RISING AND FALLING IN A SING-SONG CHANT. BELLYING FORWARD TO THE EDGE OF THE CLEARING...

...HE FOUND HANS, LYING ON HIS FACE, FEATHERED WITH ARROWS LIKE A PORCUPINE.

AT THE SAME INSTANT BUCK PEERED OUT WHERE THE SPRUCE-BOUGH LODGE HAD BEEN AND SAW WHAT MADE HIS HAIR LEAP STRAIGHT UP ON HIS NECK AND SHOULDERS.

A GUST OF OVERPOWERING RAGE SWEPT OVER HIM.

HE DID NOT KNOW THAT HE *GROWLED,* BUT HE GROWLED ALOUD WITH A *TERRIBLE FEROCITY.*

FOR THE *LAST TIME* IN HIS LIFE HE ALLOWED *PASSION* TO USURP CUNNING AND REASON, AND IT WAS FOR HIS GREAT *LOVE* OF JOHN THORNTON THAT HE LOST HIS HEAD.

THE YEEHATS HEARD A FEARFUL ROARING AND SAW RUSHING UPON THEM AN ANIMAL THE LIKE OF WHICH THEY HAD NEVER SEEN BEFORE.

> BUCK, A LIVE HURRICANE OF FURY, SPRANG AT THE YEEHAT *CHIEF* RIPPING HIS THROAT WIDE OPEN.

> WITH THE NEXT BOUND HE TORE WIDE THE THROAT OF A SECOND MAN.

THERE WAS NO WITHSTANDING HIM. HE PLUNGED ABOUT IN THEIR VERY MIDST, TEARING, RENDING, DESTROYING, IN CONSTANT AND TERRIFIC MOTION WHICH DEFIED THE ARROWS THEY DISCHARGED AT HIM.

IN FACT, SO INCONCEIVABLY RAPID WERE HIS MOVEMENTS, AND SO CLOSELY WERE THE YEEHATS TANGLED TOGETHER, THAT THEY SHOT ONE ANOTHER WITH THE ARROWS.

THEN A PANIC SEIZED THE YEEHATS, AND THEY FLED IN TERROR TO THE WOODS, PROCLAIMING AS THEY FLED THE ADVENT OF THE EVIL SPIRIT.

AND TRULY BUCK WAS THE *FIEND* INCARNATE, RAGING AT THEIR HEELS AND DRAGGING THEM DOWN LIKE DEER.

THEY SCATTERED FAR AND WIDE, AND IT WAS A WEEK LATER THAT THE *SURVIVORS* GATHERED TO COUNT THEIR LOSSES.

WEARYING OF THE *PURSUIT*, BUCK RETURNED TO THE CAMP.

134

HE FOUND *PETE*, KILLED IN THE FIRST MOMENTS OF SURPRISE.

THORNTON'S DESPERATE STRUGGLE WAS FRESH-WRITTEN ON THE EARTH, AND BUCK SCENTED EVERY DETAIL OF IT DOWN TO THE EDGE OF A DEEP POOL.

BY THE EDGE LAY *SKEET*, FAITHFUL TO THE LAST.

THE POOL, MUDDY AND DISCOLORED FROM THE SLUICE BOXES HID WHAT IT CONTAINED, AND IT CONTAINED JOHN THORNTON.

BUCK FOLLOWED HIS TRACE INTO THE WATER, FROM WHICH NO TRACE LED AWAY.

135

JOHN THORNTON'S DEATH HAD LEFT A *VOID* THAT ACHED.

IT LEFT A GREAT VOID IN HIM WHICH ACHED AND ACHED, AND WHICH FOOD COULD NOT FILL.

AT TIMES WHEN HE *PAUSED* TO CONTEMPLATE THE CARCASSES OF THE YEEHATS, HE FORGOT THE PAIN OF IT. HE WAS AWARE OF A GREAT PRIDE IN HIMSELF.

HE HAD KILLED MAN, THE *NOBLEST GAME* OF ALL, AND HAD DONE SO IN THE FACE OF THE LAW OF CLUB AND FANG.

THEY HAD DIED SO *EASILY*, IT WAS HARDER TO KILL A HUSKY.

THEY WERE *NO MATCH AT ALL*, WERE IT NOT FOR THEIR ARROWS AND SPEARS AND CLUBS.

FROM THEN ON HE WOULD BE *UNAFRAID* OF THEM EXCEPT WHEN THEY BORE IN THEIR HANDS ARROWS, SPEARS AND CLUBS.

NIGHT CAME ON, AND A *FULL MOON* ROSE HIGH OVER THE TREES.

MOURNING BY THE *POOL*, BUCK BECAME ALIVE TO A STIRRING OF THE NEW LIFE IN THE FOREST.

FROM FAR AWAY DRIFTED A FAINT, SHARP *YELP*, FOLLOWED BY A CHORUS OF SIMILAR SHARP YELPS. IT WAS THE CALL... SOUNDING MORE COMPELLINGLY THAN EVER BEFORE.

AND AS NEVER BEFORE, HE WAS READY TO OBEY. JOHN THORNTON WAS *DEAD*. THE LAST TIE WAS BROKEN.

MAN AND THE CLAIMS OF MAN NO LONGER BOUND HIM.

HUNTING THEIR MEAT, AS THE YEEHATS HAD DONE, THE *WOLF PACK* HAD INVADED BUCK'S VALLEY.

INTO THE MOONLIT *CLEARING* THEY STREAMED...

...AND IN THE CENTER STOOD *BUCK*, MOTIONLESS AS A STATUE, WAITING THEIR COMING.

THEY WERE *AWED*, SO STILL AND LARGE HE STOOD.

A MOMENT'S PAUSE FELL TILL THE *BOLDEST ONE* LEAPED FOR HIM.

LIKE A FLASH BUCK STRUCK, *BREAKING* THE NECK.

THREE OTHERS TRIED; AND ONE AFTER ANOTHER THEY *DREW BACK* WITH SLASHED THROATS OR SHOULDERS.

EAGER TO PULL DOWN THE *PREY,* THE PACK RUSHED FORWARD.

BUCK'S MARVELOUS QUICKNESS AND AGILITY STOOD HIM IN GOOD STEAD. PIVOTING ON HIS HIND LEGS, AND SNAPPING AND GASHING, HE WAS EVERYWHERE AT ONCE.

TO PREVENT THEM FROM GETTING BEHIND HIM, HE WAS *FORCED BACK,* PAST THE POOL AND INTO THE CREEK BED AND AGAINST A HIGH BANK.

HE CAME TO BAY, *PROTECTED* ON THREE SIDES WITH NOTHING TO DO BUT FACE FRONT.

SO WELL DID HE FACE IT, THAT THE WOLVES *DREW BACK,* TONGUES LOLLING AND FANGS FLASHING IN THE MOONLIGHT.

THEY WATCHED AS *ONE WOLF,* LONG AND LEAN, ADVANCED IN A *FRIENDLY* MANNER.

BUCK RECOGNIZED THE *WILD BROTHER* WITH WHOM HE HAD RUN FOR A NIGHT AND DAY.

AN *OLD WOLF*, GAUNT AND BATTLE-SCARRED, CAME FORWARD.

BUCK WRITHED HIS LIPS TO SNARL, BUT INSTEAD *SNIFFED NOSES* WITH HIM.

WHEREUPON THE OLD WOLF SAT DOWN, POINTED NOSE AT THE MOON, AND BROKE
OUT THE LONG *HOWL.*

THE OTHERS SAT
DOWN AND HOWLED.

NOW THE *CALL* CAME TO
BUCK. HE, TOO, SAT
DOWN AND HOWLED.

THE *LEADERS* LIFTED THE YELP OF THE PACK AND SPRANG INTO THE WOODS.

THE WOLVES SWUNG IN BEHIND, *YELPING* IN CHORUS.

BUCK RAN WITH THEM, *SIDE BY SIDE* WITH THE WILD BROTHER, YELPING AS HE RAN.

HERE MAY END THE *STORY* OF BUCK.

BUT THE YEEHATS TELL OF A *GHOST DOG,* THAT RUNS AT THE HEAD OF THE PACK. THEY ARE AFRAID OF THIS GHOST DOG, FOR IT HAS CUNNING GREATER THAN THEY.

IT *STEALS* FROM THEIR TRAPS, *SLAYS* THEIR DOGS AND *DEFIES* THEIR BRAVEST HUNTERS.

NAY, THE TALE GROWS WORSE.

HUNTERS HAVE BEEN FOUND WITH *SLASHED THROATS* AND PRINTS ABOUT THEM IN THE SNOW, GREATER THAN ANY WOLF.

EACH FALL, WHEN THEY FOLLOW THE MOOSE,

THERE IS A CERTAIN *VALLEY* THE YEEHATS NEVER ENTER.

AND *WORD* GOES OVER THE FIRE...

...OF HOW THE *EVIL SPIRIT* CAME TO SELECT THAT VALLEY FOR AN ABIDING-PLACE.

IN THE SUMMERS THERE IS *ONE VISITOR* TO THAT VALLEY OF WHICH THE YEEHATS DO NOT KNOW.

HE CROSSES *ALONE,* THIS GREAT WOLF LIKE NO OTHER WOLVES...

...AND COMES TO AN *OPEN SPACE* AMONG THE TREES.

HERE A YELLOW STREAM FLOWS FROM ROTTED MOOSE-HIDE SACKS AND SINKS INTO THE GROUND.

HE MUSES HERE, *HOWLING ONCE,* LONG AND MOURNFULLY BEFORE HE DEPARTS.

BUT HE IS *NOT ALONE*.

WHEN THE *WINTER* COMES, AND THE WOLVES HUNT IN THE *VALLEY*, HE MAY BE SEEN RUNNING THROUGH THE PALE MOONLIGHT.

...HIS GREAT THROAT A-BELLOW AS HE SINGS A *SONG* OF THE YOUNGER WORLD...

...WHICH IS THE SONG OF THE PACK.

THE END

THE MAKING OF

JACK LONDON'S

THE CALL OF THE WILD

"Good writers drop their characters into treacherous
territory and force them to adapt. I can't think of a
more treacherous territory than London's tundra . . .
and a more adaptable protagonist than Buck."
—Neil Kleid

NEIL KLEID
TALKS ABOUT HIS ADAPTATION OF

JACK LONDON'S

Dogs are people too.

I learned that the hard way when I agreed to adapt *The Call of the Wild*. Telling a story from a dog's point of view was extremely tricky, especially since most of my past work relied heavily on sarcastic and often comedic dialogue. For one, there's the "animals can't speak" thing. Second, I tend to research dialogue patterns when crafting a story and, well . . . it's hard to follow a dog around all day, listening to barking, hoping to find motivation or narration for a story about nature, loyalty, roots, survival, and love.

London was smart—he went the novel route, where it's easier to get inside a dog's head. His narrative is packed with Buck's thoughts and emotions, explaining a deep, layered bond between the elemental pack dog, his mates and his master. But in a graphic novel? Unless you're turning Buck into a Grant Morrison-esque cybernetic soldier, there's only one option for effective communication: narrative captions.

Early in the process I discovered one advantage the graphic novel format offered me vis-à-vis Buck's communication skills—visual action. Just like human protagonists, Buck could express himself through movement and overall body language. I did my best to tell London's wonderful story utilizing the strength of the medium, letting Alex Niño's beautiful artwork enhance my narration of Jack London's incredible tale of one dog's journey across the frozen North.

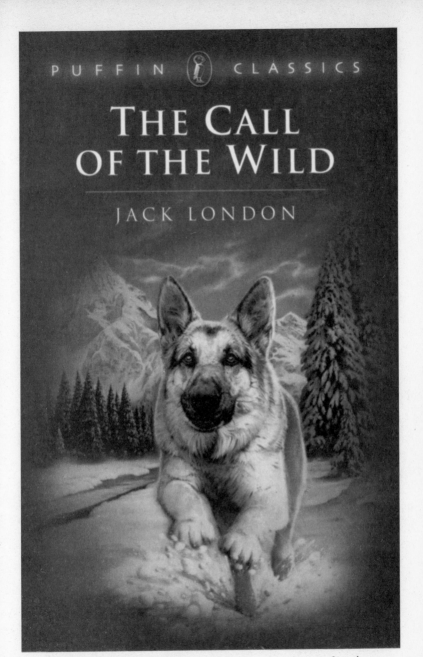

The Puffin Classics edition that was the source for the graphic novel adaptation.

ALEX NIÑO'S
COVER SKETCH GALLERY

Alex Niño drew three cover sketches for the cover to the graphic novel.

COVER STUDY FOR `CALL OF THE WILD´ (2)

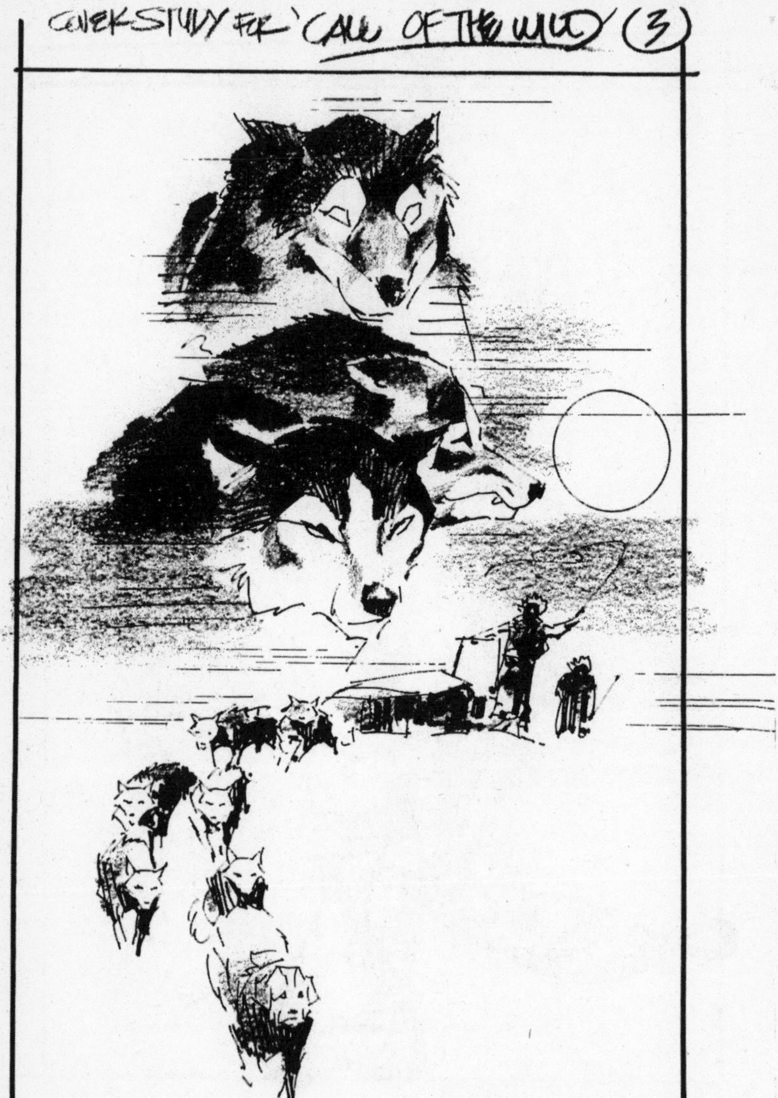
COVER STUDY FOR 'CALL OF THE WILD' (3)

ALEX NIÑO'S SKETCH GALLERY

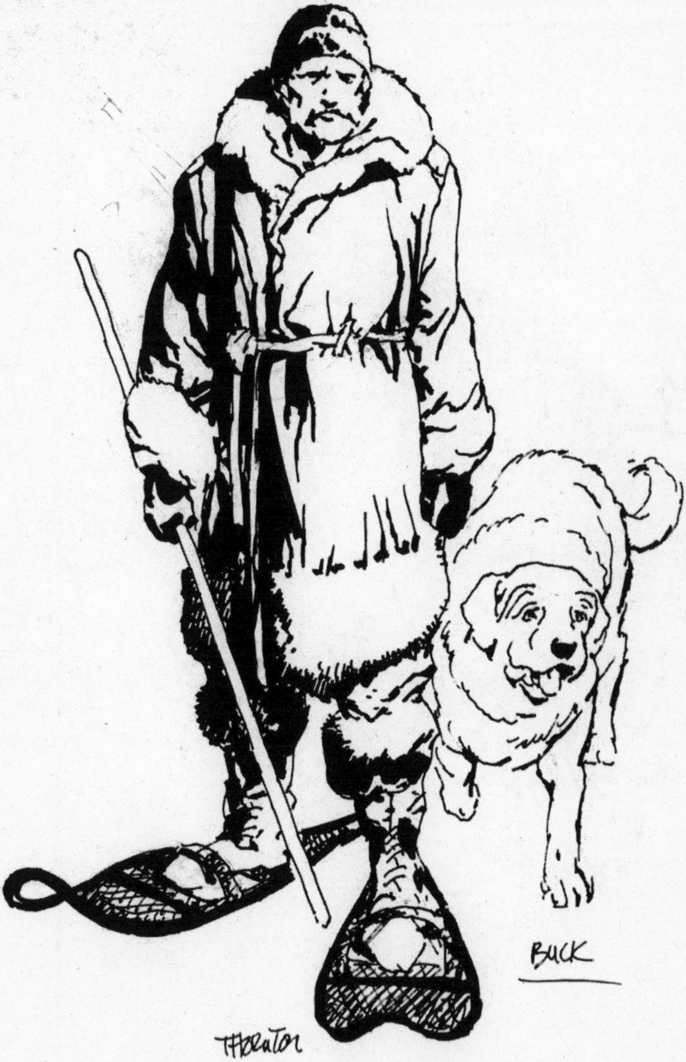
BUCK
THORNTON

BUCK

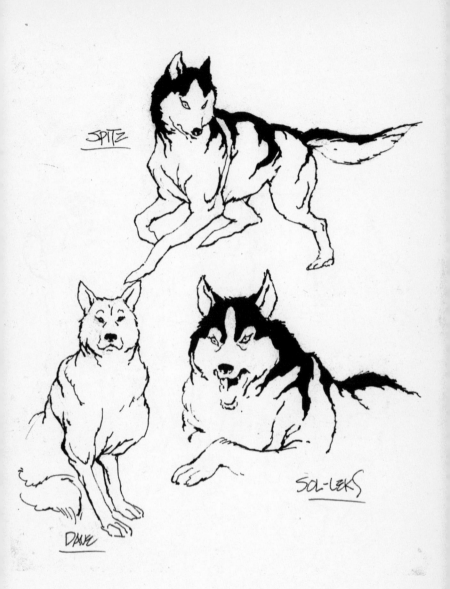

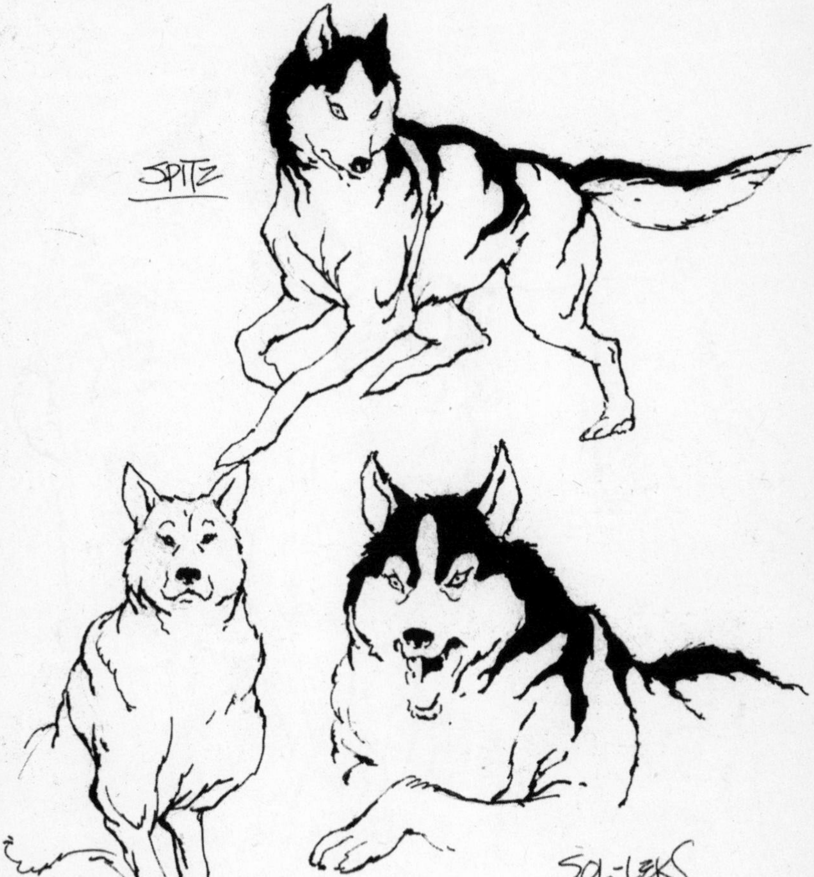
SPITZ
DAVE
SOL-LEKS

CURLY

<u>Page 11 (4 PANELS)</u>

PAGE LAYOUT: Three tiered panels, each running the length of the page.

PANEL ONE
Buck breaks free of the crate, launching himself at the man. Mouth foaming and a cold glitter in his bloodshot eyes, it looks like Buck has gone rabid.

PANEL TWO
The man swings his arm up and catches Buck on the muzzle with the club.

NARRATIVE CAP:

> HE HAD NEVER FELT A CLUB BEFORE, AND
> SHOCK CLOSED HIS MUZZLE IN AGONIZING PAIN.

PANEL THREE
Buck goes down to the ground on his back and side, shocked.

NARRATIVE CAP:

> THE CLUB BROKE BUCK'S CHARGE AND
> MADNESS BROUGHT HIM BACK FOR MORE.

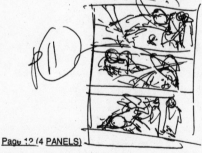

<u>Page 12 (4 PANELS)</u>

PAGE LAYOUT: Four panels – three tiers. The top two tiers extend the length of

The first step many comics artists use in developing the art for a graphic novel is to create thumbnail sketches of the script. Here are a selection of pages of Neil Kleid's script showing Alex Niño's thumbnail sketches drawn on them.

NARRATIVE CAP:

THEY WERE WISE IN THE WAY OF DOGS AND
FAIR TO JUDGE.

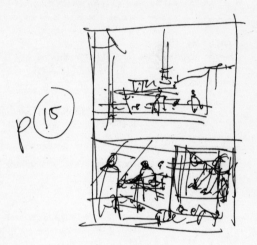

P (15)

Page 16 (3 PANELS)

PAGE LAYOUT: Three tiered panels, each running the length of the page.

PANEL ONE
INT – THE NARWHAL
Buck and Curly prowl along the long decks of the Narwhal, passing crates and
crewmen. The other two dogs walk ahead of them, one proud and imperious
and the other with his head down. The proud dog ventures into the next cabin.

NARRATIVE CAP:

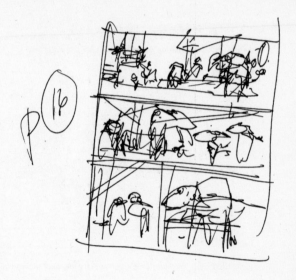

Page 17 (3 PANELS)

PAGE LAYOUT: Three tiered panels, each running the length of the page.

PANEL ONE
INT. NARWHAL- MORNING
Francois leans down and attaches a leash to Buck's neck.

NARRATIVE CAP:

> THE DAYS PASSED, AND BUCK FELT THE AIR
> TURN COLDER.

trail. We are looking up, over their shoulders to a vast mountain range, endless trees and the hints of the frozen Lake Bennet. This is the Yukon – with the call of the wild and adventure lying just beneath duty, toil and winter's chill.

NARRATIVE CAP:

AND THOUGH THE WORK WAS HARD —

NARRATIVE CAP:

—BUCK FOUND THAT HE DID NOT HATE IT.

Page 28 (3 PANELS)

PAGE LAYOUT: Three tiered panels, each running the length of the page.

PANEL ONE
Close on the dogs – Buck is placed between Dave (behind him) and Sol-Leks (in front). He's being "instructed" by Dave's teeth and Francois' whip.

NARRATIVE CAP:

HE WAS PLACED BETWEEN DAVE AND SOL-LEKS TO RECEIVE INSTRUCTION.

NARRATIVE CAP:

THEY WERE FAIR AND WISE, AS WAS FRANCOIS WHIP.

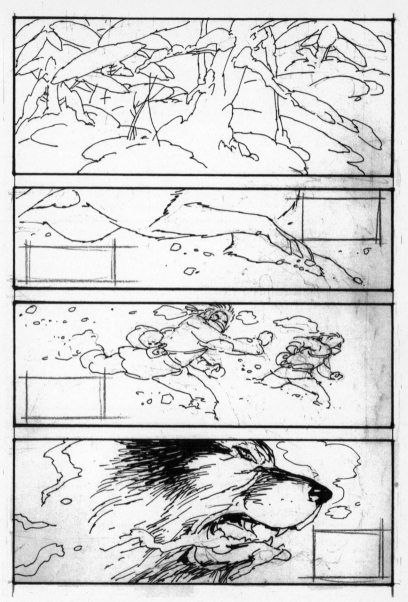

Here is a twelve-page sequence from the beginning of the story. The rectangular boxes are Alex Niño's placement suggestions for the text.

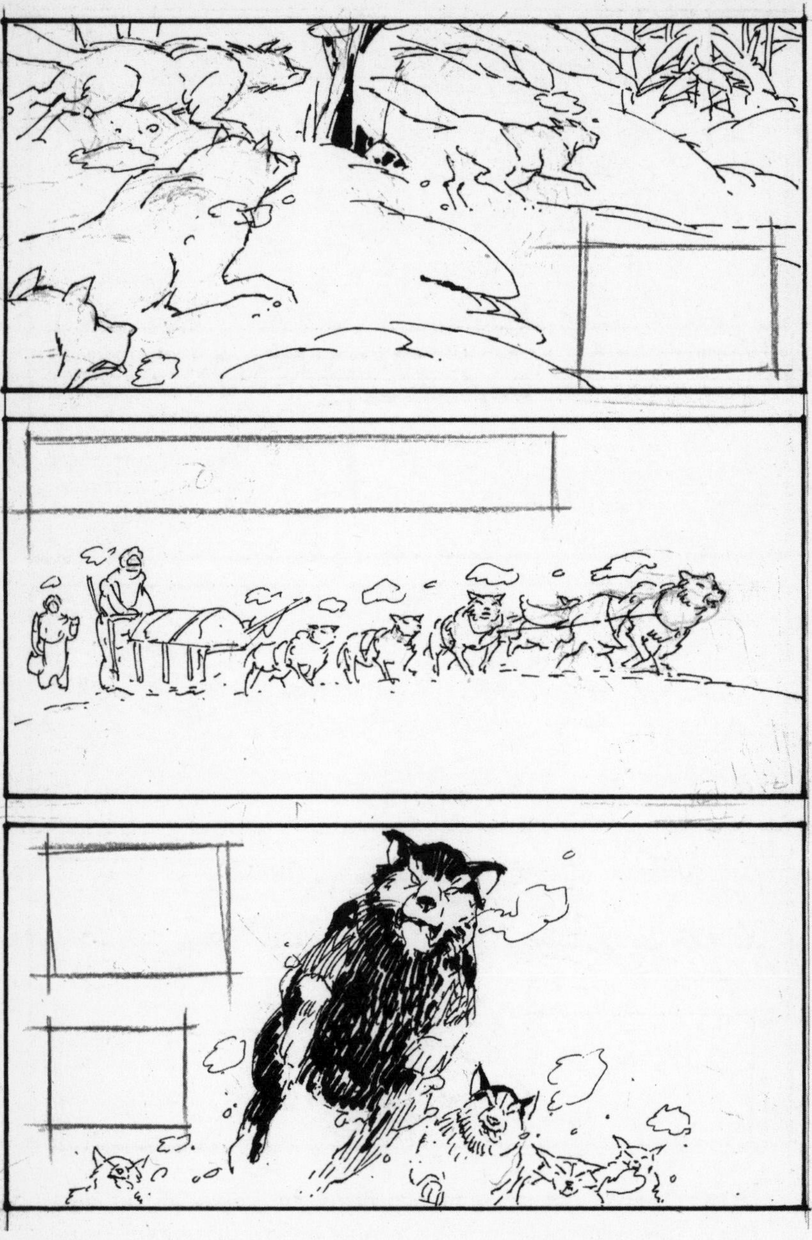

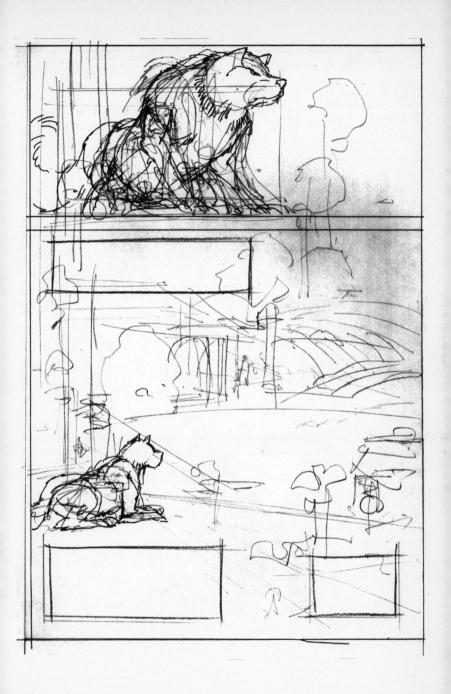

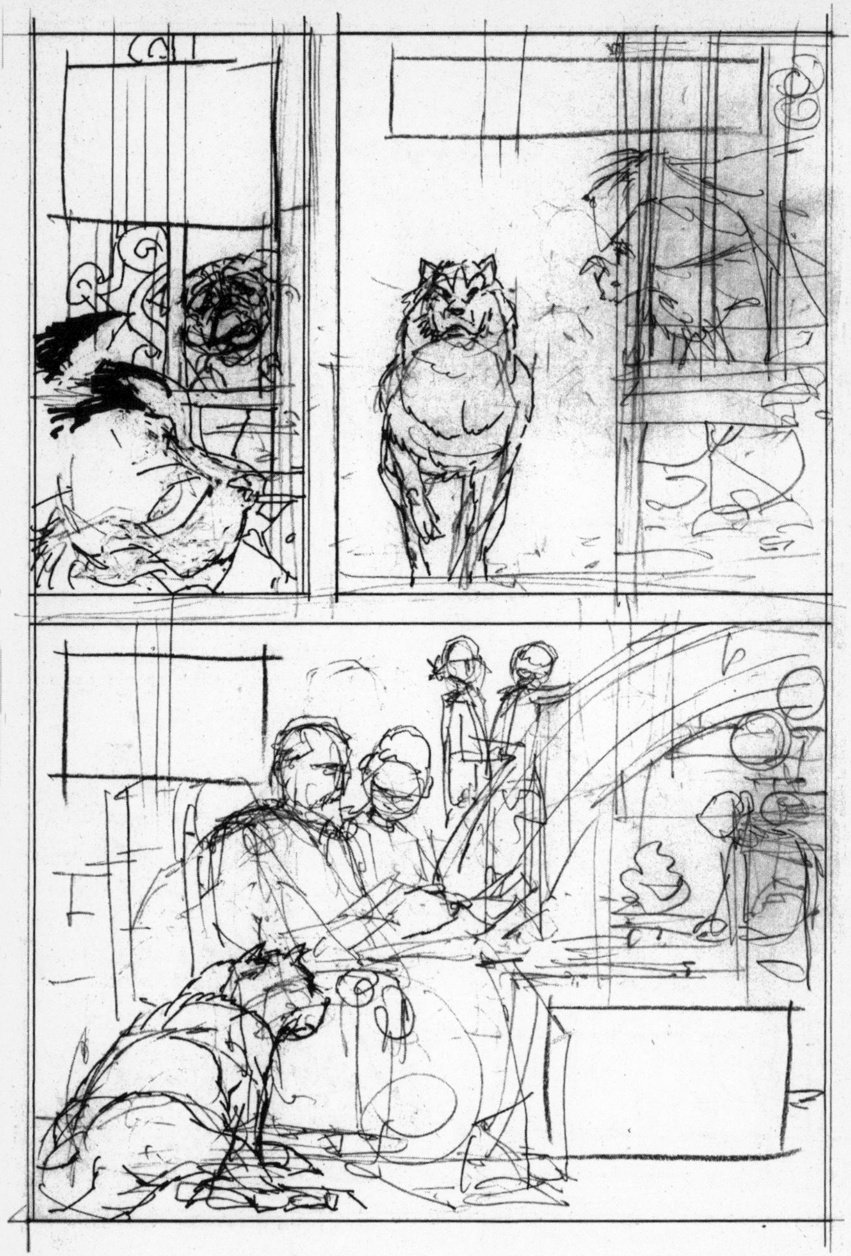

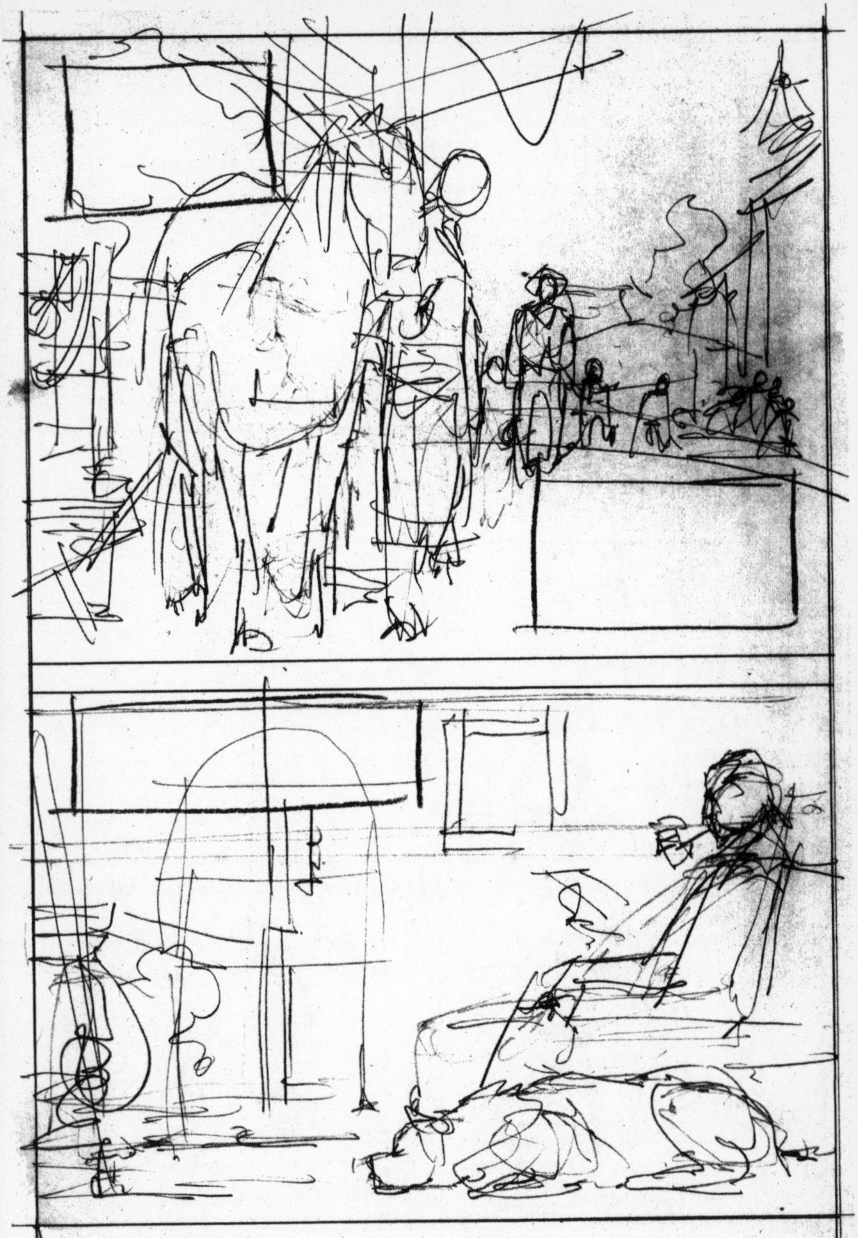

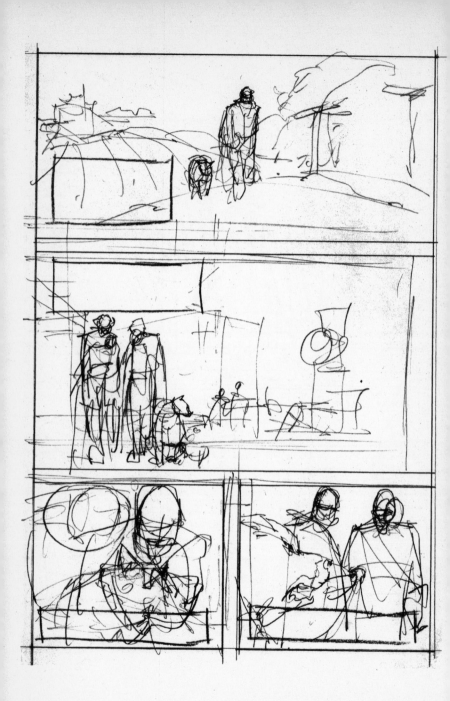

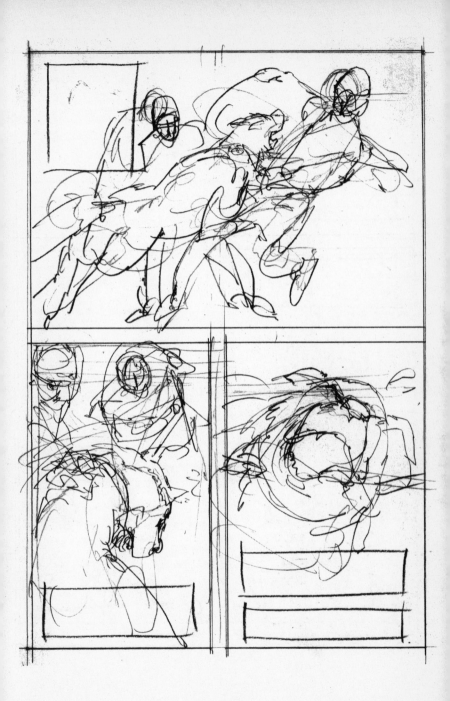

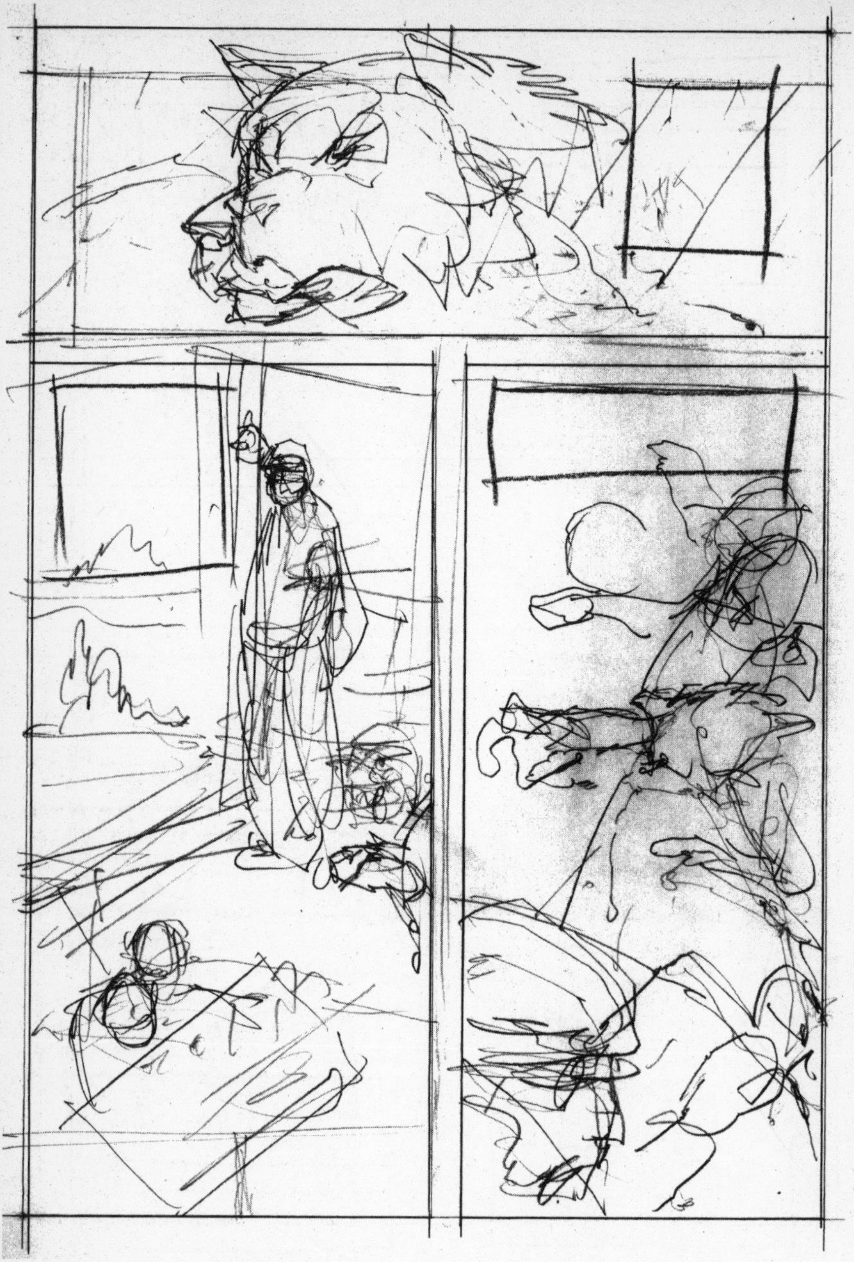

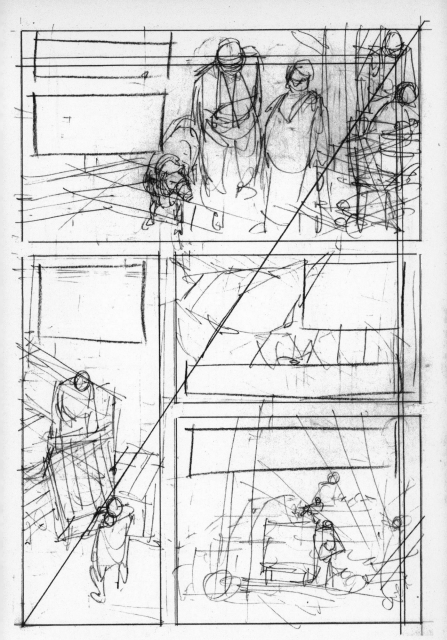

Alex drew the long diagonal line on this page as a check
to make sure his artwork was proportional to the printed
page size.

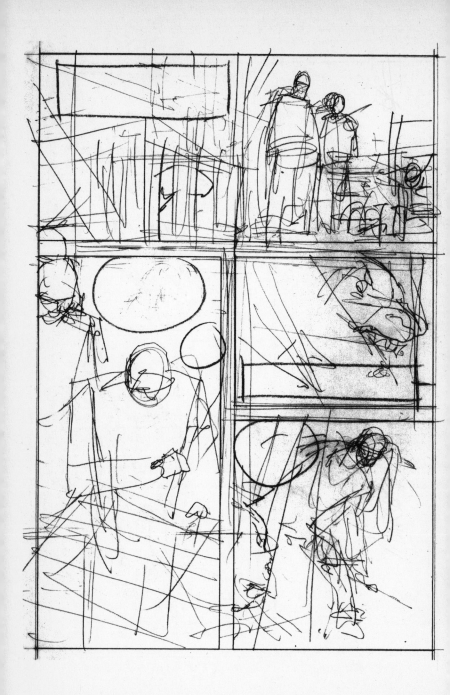

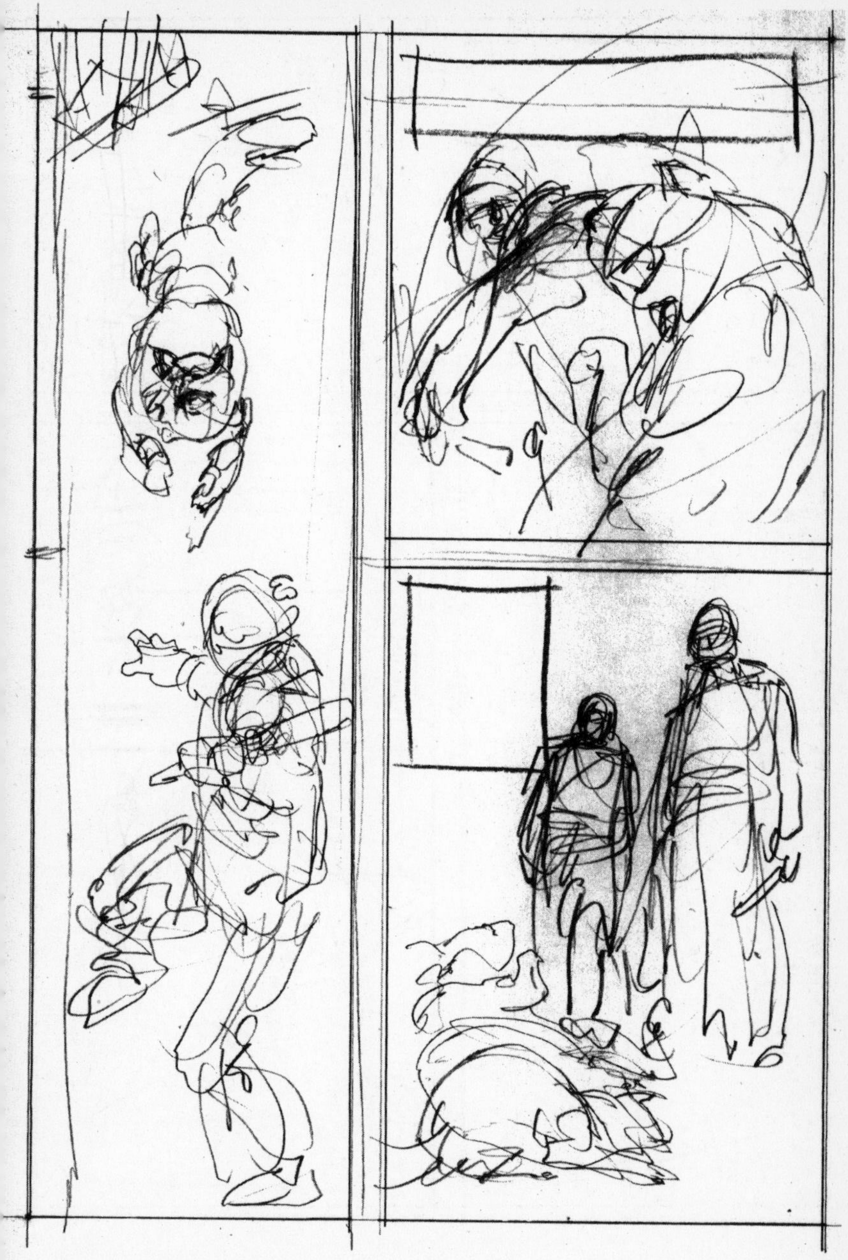

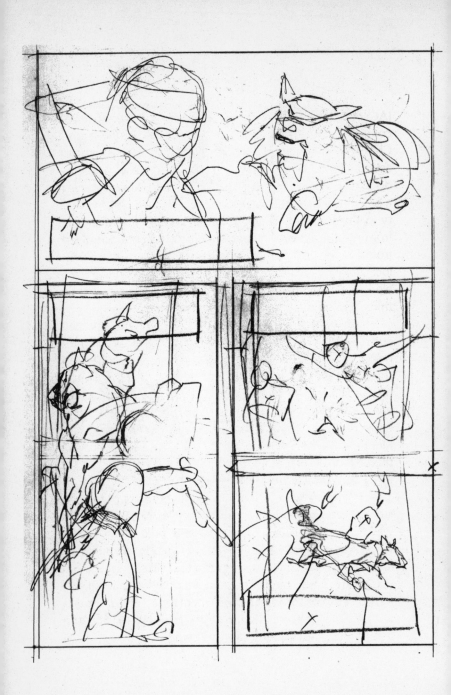

JACK LONDON (1876–1916) led a life that could have come out of one of his adventure stories. He was born John Chaney, the illegitimate son of an itinerant Irish-American astrologer and Flora Wellman, the black sheep of a well-to-do family. Before Jack was one year old, Flora had married a grocer called John London and settled into a life of poverty in Pennsylvania. Young Jack increasingly found escape from the grimness of his surroundings in books borrowed from the local library; his reading was guided by a kindly local librarian. When he was fifteen, he left home and traveled around North America as a tramp. He once served thirty days in prison on a charge of vagrancy.

By the time Jack was nineteen, he could drink and curse as well as his fellow boatmen in California, but he never lost his love of reading. His socialist creed stressed the importance of education and by dint of cramming all his lost schooling into a few months, he managed to gain entry into the University of California. He soon left, however, and in 1896 was caught up in the gold rush to the Klondike River in northwest Canada. He returned from there with no gold at all, but with the seed of a story that in 1903 became a huge best seller, *The Call of the Wild.*

This was followed in 1906 by his other popular dog story *White Fang,* and by many other books. By 1913 he was the highest-paid and most widely read writer in the world. He spent all his money on his friends, on drinking, and especially on building himself a castlelike house, which was destroyed by fire before completion. Financial difficulties forced him to drive himself mercilessly, and he drank heavily. Finally, he could stand no more and in 1916, at the age of forty, Jack London took his own life.

NEIL KLEID was born in Detroit, Michigan. He won a Xeric Grant for *Ninety Candles,* a graphic novella about life, fatherhood, comics, and death, and wrote *Brownsville,* a graphic novel about Murder Incorporated, with artist Jake Allen. He's authored several minicomics and has contributed stories to various magazines and anthologies over the years. Neil is currently writing *Ursa Minors!,* a creator-owned miniseries for Slave Labor Graphics, and an ongoing superhero series for Jim Valentino's Shadowline imprint at Image Comics. He currently resides in New York City where he hopes to write more dog stories.

ALEX NIÑO is a Filipino comics artist acclaimed for his remarkable versatility and originality. He worked as a photographer and musician before breaking into comics in his native Philippines in 1965. His first story for the U.S. market appeared in *Weird Heroes* #6 in 1977. Alex has worked for DC Comics, Marvel Comics, and numerous other publishers. He currently lives in Van Nuys, California.